ASHEN SHADOWS

ASHEN SHADOWS

Print edition ISBN: 9798649200035
Copyright © Ewe Linka

First paperback edition: July 2020
Independently published

Character art by Ellie Lin
Instagram: @kynerie

ASHEN SHADOWS

by Ewe Linka

TO MY GRANDAD

from my first steps
to his last

PROLOGUE

Darkness draped peculiar shadows over the walls. A climbing rose vine curved around the windows, rooted down by rusty chains, stems reaching up towards the peak of the highest tower, and the edges of its leaves yellow and crumpled. The stairs were steep and illuminated only by a faint touch of the full moon. Unshackling the chain guarding the door, he found the old chest, stashed away under dusty paintings and empty, ripped scrolls. Only then did he dare to light a lantern held in his left hand, setting it aside below the chipped windowsill.

Except for his creaky steps, there was a silent void.

He tugged at a rusty key to force the chest open, battling with its squeaky hinges. Then, he reached inside for a bundle of letters, wrapped with a rough brown twine. He leaned against the wall with his back, ready to unravel the first letter. His rough hand glided across the parchment, smoothing out the crease lines, and focused his eyes on the dappled ink.

Dear Akela,

When we welcome you into the world, you will be the most powerful princess of them all. No other kingdom will have your powers as their weapon, and that's what worries me a great deal. I can't sleep thinking about the amount of havoc Isla can cause with you under her wing. If you turn out to have MY powers, there will be no stopping her.

Therefore, forgive me for what I'm about to do, but spending time with Isla last night confirmed my worries, and I want you to have no part in whatever she thinks will happen when you're born.

The evening was the same as any other. I sat in the very chair I'm sitting in right now with the fireplace crackling dangerously loud in my ears, shattering my confidence into mere specks of dust. And it makes me uneasy, causing me to shift. Isla, with the crown entwined around her head, joined me in the library, her hand laid on you the entire time, making sure you're comfortable.

Unlike me.

"How long will you be here?" she asked, but I knew it wasn't a question. It was a demand to put my book away and follow her into our – her – chambers where we used to make love.

Now, the chamber is riddled with dusty residue of whatever love meant. Crawling away from our hearts.

My father once said, 'Nothing lasts forever', and I'd be damned to ever agree with him, but this time, I must.

Falling in love with Isla was the worst thing a man could ever do. She gripped me in her claws and now I can't leave.

Not until your face sees the light of day, not until you hold my thumb with all of your tiny fingers, not until I whisk you away from the cruelty the Valeis land gained. I must get us out of here; as far as it is safe, because the last thing I want for you is to become your mother.

"Just a minute, love," I replied, keeping up the pretences. Whatever to make her happy. After all, she controls half of the kingdom's common folk and not me.

Folding the edge of the page I was on to keep my place, I put the book down and followed her through the corridors.

I couldn't walk beside her, no. Her dress was so puffy from the waist down, there was hardly any space near her. I watched as the hems dusted the floors until the grim corridor turned into our bedchamber. A maid tipped a teapot over two clay mugs and I reached for them both, passing one to Isla as she took off the bottom part of her dress. The maid scurried about, picking up discarded clothing, neatly folding it away.

A silk underdress was lifted slightly at the front to give space to you, growing inside a hateful woman. I stared at the contents of my mug for a moment longer, although I didn't dare drink from it.

Isn't a woman's greatest weapon poison?

At least that's what my father told me, not long before his fifth wife tipped something into his drink. I saw it. I didn't say anything.

After the maid left our chamber and there was nothing for me to do, other than pretend to still be smitten with

11

your mother; that sorrowful woman who would do anything to hurt me – to take my powers away for her own, if only she could. I rested my hand on the bump where you lay, dropped my trousers to satisfy Isla enough for her to finally give in and fall asleep.

Seconds before she fell asleep, she whispered, almost softly, "With our precious daughter, we will be unstoppable." She knew you were going to be born a girl; it runs in the family, she told me.

And when she said 'we', it didn't include me because the words were filled with greed. I knew that the moment you were born, you would grow up without a father. You would grow up with Isla and live by everything she believed was right. Without me.

And it pained me to imagine the day.

I counted down the days until you were born hoping they would never end.

Neatly, he folded the letter and placed it back inside the chest. Curiosity had a way of pushing him into collecting scraps of knowledge – knowledge that one day may get him killed. The light within him shone brighter as he reached for the second letter, his nose catching wafts of dust from the musky parchment. Finding these memories of life helped him to understand what had really happened within those castle walls, giving him something beyond just knowledge. In a twisted way, it offered him the hope of a way out.

A gentle thud of his heart didn't let him forget he shouldn't be here. The key to the chamber belonged to Queen Isla, but he managed to whisk it away and sneak in unnoticed. Many of his tricks lay beneath the surface of a pretty face – the ability to coax people into doing whatever he willed.

Something rattled, scraping against the floor, then barged into a pile of the farmost boxes, barrels and crates. His heart raced. He breathed out slowly, calming. Mice, stumbling across the floor, dragged the door chain. Getting up and securely tying the chain to the lock, he sat back down again, this time on top of one of the crates. The second letter, although written in the same scrawny cursive, felt different.

Dear Akela,

When you grow up, you will learn a few things.

After the age of thirteen, your eyes will change colour. They won't stay grey forever. That will help you go unnoticed in crowds. Not everyone will have to know you are Drishti, unless you show them.

When I used my magic for the first time, and I'm going to be completely honest with you, I had no clue what I was doing, but it was the most natural thing I ever experienced. I looked into the eyes of an older kid who was throwing pebbles at cattle, where I was helping a local farmer in exchange for some food and milk. I looked into his eyes, and I remember to this day the way his smug face snarled and mocked me, until the pebbles fell from his grasp, scattering by his feet.

It was like magic flew right through my veins and into his mind. I knew he was going to do whatever I told him to do, but as I saw a flicker of fear flash across his face, all I did was tell him to go away and never bother any animals again. Invading someone's mind was beyond intrusive. I swore to myself I would only use my powers if I had no other choice.

The moment everything changed for me, I was walking down the same old path into Zeffari's Keep from the farm I worked at, back home, back to my family; your grandmother whom you'll never meet. It turned out, after I left, she was not the lucky one.

I was stopped by a pair of guards, their heads held high and the hilts of their swords shining in the sun, almost blinding me when I dared a glimpse at them. I thought being Drishti gave me immunity. But it wasn't them who discovered I was Drishti, it was, at the time, Princess Isla herself.

Behind the guards, was a carriage, lined with a royal red carpet within and on the steps outside; bolted down with thick nails. I might have paid too much attention to the corner of one of the steps where the nail appeared to be sticking out slightly.

A snicker escaped one of the horse's mouths and I saw a pale hand, full of shimmering rings, creep out of the carriage. My eyes fell onto her leg. She quickly covered it up bringing the fabric of her dress over her naked skin. My attention flew up to her face, cheeks that gained a prominent splash of red as her eyes fell upon mine.

I'm not going to tell you that I hated her from the beginning, because I didn't. I was infatuated with her. She was beautiful and what was I if not a common boy of simple pleasures?

She looked at me with a shy smile and I instinctively bowed my head, dropping my gaze to the ground, until she told me to raise it up again and look at her.

"You're beautiful," I choked out before remembering I was speaking to a princess. I found out I misspoke the moment one of the guards elbowed me in the ribs and I doubled over before her.

She quickly scolded the man, finding her way to my side and helping me stand straight up again. I could see worry skim her features, but I didn't know it was all an act. Her eyes locked with mine and I felt she was trying to connect with me, but she was met with an impenetrable barrier.

She smiled again, knowing I was Drishti. There was a hint of mystery in that smile of hers, and I was intrigued. Could she have known back then that I had powers that extended beyond a simple compulsion of humans? Could she have seen it in my eyes, even then? But these were not the questions my mind was filled with. I was sixteen and to have been noticed by a princess was beyond my greatest expectations.

Her hand flew up to my hair and she ruffled through it, her palm resting on my cheek for a brief moment like a delicate butterfly kiss. She asked, "Are you okay?"

To tell you the truth, I was more than okay.
And that's how it all began.

With the third and final letter, his hands shook as he read it, realising he might be the only person, except for Queen Isla herself and whoever had written this letter, that knew what really happened to Akela.

He swallowed, folded the letter up and stashed it away into the folds of his fur-lined coat, leaving the tower, locking and chaining the door tight behind him and sneaking back into the midst of the castle.

six years ago

Ezme sat on the roof of a small wooden cabin she called home, surrounded by vast Esteracre woods, spreading over the southeast border of the land of Valeis, her feet dangling over the edge. She could feel the magic inside her stirring awake, slowly stuttering to life, warming her chest, stretching its limbs after a long, deep sleep. She took a deep breath in, willing it to break free, but she knew it was not the time just yet.

As she breathed out, thin ribbons of mist released from her mouth, floating up until a wisp of cool air blew it away. She clutched a jar of fireflies closer to her chest, hiding its light within the confines of her scuffed coat at the sound of footsteps. She stared into the darkness below, measuring her breath in prolonged paces.

A slow, feeble whistle reached her numb ears, relaxing her shoulders as she gave a deep sigh, letting out her breath again, feeling the warmth of the mist curl up to her cheeks. Tentatively, she listened as the snow crunched under a pair of boots mixing with the swift rustling of tree branches and the distant howl of a wolf.

She couldn't see much as she inched carefully forward, her head tipping over the ledge, one hand curling its fingers over the sharp edge of the wooden plank. A soft whisper on her lips called out his name, "Oliver?"

They met every fortnight. Ezme would wait up for Oliver until he finally showed up, sneaking away from his house. Sometimes she would wait for hours before returning back inside to lay her head on the pillow, ready to give up, exhausted from staring into the distance and hoping to see a flicker of light or hear a familiar voice. He would often collect a few stones to throw at her window, careful not to shatter it. Small, but loud enough to get her attention so that she could slip away into the night with him.

For her safety, Ezme wasn't allowed out because she wasn't ordinary – she wasn't like Oliver who could just prowl around every nook and cranny of the kingdom without a worry. He was a kid and she desperately wanted to be a normal kid too, able to do the things that he could. If her father found out she had made a friend beyond the confines of the Esteracre cabin…

But she knew two things.

First, there was much more to life than hiding.

Second, she trusted Oliver. She trusted he understood how getting caught could jeopardise not only her safety, but the safety of all the other kids in the cabin with her.

She threw the jar of fireflies down as he extended his arms out, a gleam of buzzing lights illuminated the almond shade of his face, revealing a boyish smile. After he placed the jar on the front step, he jerked his head sideways before she leapt forward. Her weight crashed into him, pinning him to the ground, elbow digging into his ribs.

"That was rather graceful," he moaned, then pushed her off to the side and stood up quickly, adjusting the folds of his coat. It was a size too big for him, but soon he would grow into it.

She grabbed onto his hand to find her footing, dusting herself off from the snow.

"It's freezing! Where's your hat?"

She scrunched her nose. "Forgot."

Jamming his own woolly hat on top of her head, he explained at the sight of her lips pursing, ready to protest, "I've got gloves." She didn't. It was always that simple with him.

On the verge of the trees surrounding the lonely cabin was a fire torch impaled into the snow. Oliver picked it up, illuminating their way past a narrow plateau of dying, dry cedars, the weight of the snow breaking their weaker branches. The bigger branches were covered in small prints of birds who managed to find shelter in the hollow of the bark. An oak tree, at least a hundred years old, had a hole in the higher part of the bark where an owl sat and flickered its big, unmoving eyes at them, close to the open field from which an array of small villages were piled, some with candles in their windows, and most with their drapes tightly drawn.

"That is not creepy at all," she whispered, looping her arm through his.

"Don't tell me you're still scared of that little owl."

"I'm telling you, that owl is—"

"A wise and magnificent creature?"

She frowned. "I was going to say dangerous and up to no good."

"So, just like you then?"

She let out a long breath, rolling her eyes at him. "Look at it and its murderous eyes! It's definitely planning something vicious."

As soon as the words left her lips, the owl took flight, diving to clasp a small creature in its deadly sharp claws. Ezme shuddered at the sound of a squeak, shaking her head as she pulled away from Oliver's arm.

"And what did I tell you?"

All he did was laugh.

Snow fell faster and thicker by the minute as they marched on until they reached an empty path surrounded by a row of fire torches, crackling and swaying whatever direction the wind dictated. A fresh breeze swept Oliver's ash brown hair over his eyes, the hollow sound of shimmering branches dispersed around them, whistling loudly.

Ezme leaned against one of the trees and realised he was glancing at her with a hint of unearthed curiosity, shuffling from one foot to the other. She'd never seen him so anxious before.

"Is it midnight yet?" she asked him.

He inspected her face carefully, squinting, inches from her nose. "Not yet, I don't see a change."

"Then stop staring at me like that," she snapped, but her gaze hadn't left his.

Instead, she kept her head levelled, darting between his bushy eyebrows and expectant eyes, pressing her lips into a thin impatient line.

Waiting for something to happen.

Willing for midnight to strike sooner.

She could feel it. The tips of her fingers were tingling so she grabbed hold of the frayed hems of her sleeves, her breath shortening in anticipation.

She knew it was happening the moment Oliver's mouth fell open and he took an uneven step back. There was no sign of fear; his eyes never left hers, continuing to dwell deep in a daze. Her usual sharp grey shade whirled and, as she blinked, he saw her pupils dilate, turning into dark, but warm pools of hazelnut.

With his throat suddenly dry, it took him two tries before he was able to swallow and mutter, "Your...eyes. It happened."

Despite a trickling coldness seeping under her scarf, she beamed, a giggle playing on her lips as she brought him closer into an embrace.

"Happy thirteenth birthday, Ez. Make a wish."

"No more hiding," she willed as they separated at the Crossroads, a certain skip accompanying her steps.

The shortest way was past a local tavern called 'The Honey Brew' where most of the common folk spent their afternoons leading deep into the night at. The tavern was humming with voices and a cheery tune strung from a badly tuned lute. The ale spilled over the pitchers and people yelled over one another while playing cards at the tables. The fogged glass in the windows threatened to burst and shatter into pieces.

The jingle of coins was what made Blade focus, what made her tick, her eyes piercing through the oversized bellies of men who ate and drank their way into the next day. She only needed a few coins to feed herself and gather warmer clothes. She didn't need much.

She waited in the shadows of the tavern, unnoticed, before she followed one of the men outside. He hiccupped as he unbuckled his trousers next to a tree, releasing a satisfying hum. He was unaware when Blade snatched the satchel with coins from his pocket.

The moment she took a step, the satchel slipped from her fingers and clinked on the ground by his feet. The man turned, doing his trousers up quickly, and grabbed her by the collar of her shirt as she tried to scramble for the satchel. With his other hand he grasped the coins from her and shoved them back into his pocket.

"You think you can scam me? You pathetic little girl!" he chortled and just as quickly a smug grin appeared on his puffy face. "I'll show you what we do with thieving girls like you around here."

He coughed, wheezing slightly through his nose, slinging the belt out from the loops of his trousers and holding it halved, ready. He bent her over and was about to strike with the metal grip when someone whistled and yelled at the top of their lungs.

As he turned to see who it was, Ezme's hazelnut eyes flicked grey, piercing through his small drunken slits, and a warm wave filled her body. She felt the power reach every nerve like the buzz of a hundred bees. Taking a deeper breath, she penetrated the depths of his mind, easing herself into complete control over him. The belt fell from his grip and he let go of Blade's collar, shuffling clumsily back into the tavern, almost tripping over the step, and leaving the two girls behind.

"You're Drishti…" Blade muttered, shaking her head in disbelief. "You shouldn't be here; you should be hiding."

A silver mist escaped Blade's nostrils as she took in sharp gasps of air. She shivered, crossing her hands over her shoulders, rubbing them down all the way to her elbows in an energetic motion to keep warm. Her lip began to turn blue. Ezme unbuttoned her coat and offered it to her without a second thought.

"You think I need your help?" Blade snarled, stepping out of the shadow of the tree, letting the moonlight hit her face. There was a nail scratch on the side of her neck. Fresh. "I would have handled that drunken bastard just fine and because of you, he's taken the coins with him!"

A sharp piece of silverware slid down the inside of her arm, gleaming at them in a daring, ready-to-slash, promise.

Ezme took one step back, but held her coat out in front, her brows knitting together in both defiance and confusion. "I just wanted to help. Take my coat, I have a few coins in one of the pockets. Have them. Please."

A hollow snigger filled the suffocating space between them. "You think you're better than me, is that so? Just because you have a roof above your head and family to go home to every night? Clean clothes that smell of fresh linen from a mile away? And an oh-so-useful power that can just as easily get you killed?" Blade walked up to Ezme, shoving the coat back into her arms, enjoying the startled look on her face and a trembling lip. "Go back into hiding, cursed child."

"I–I–didn't—"

And just like that, Blade was gone.

The sound of the strings from the tavern dulled out and the loud, monotonous conversations echoed long after Ezme returned home, shuffling her bare feet under a sheep skin, her shoulders still shivering in memory of the encounter.

PART
I

CHAPTER 1

The sky hung troubled with dark clouds, the full moon reflecting upon the earth guiding moths towards the lanterns suspended beside every wooden door. The gravel paths were empty, except for the whistling swish penetrating the crevices in the windows.

Ezme felt the cold, mizzling droplets of rain on her nose. Her coat swung heavy on her shoulders as she sped to the end of the Crossroads village. The edge of Esteracre woods growled as she stood still for a while, listening. Her lower lip trembled as she sucked air in through her mouth, setting off into the darkness ahead. Through thick, wet eyelashes she saw a glimmer of light; a warm, cascading glow.

"Queen Isla is killing again," she said, pulling the hood down from the top of her head as soon as she pushed past Oliver in the doorway. The creak resonated through the hinges until he shut it tight behind her, sliding the metal lock into place.

She took her coat off and flung it onto a chair, water trickling down from it. Muddy footprints ran all the way to the far wall before she took her boots off.

"Where?" he asked calmly, not a drop of surprise within his voice, proceeding to light a few more beeswax candles on the table.

A musky blend of warm vanilla and invigorating cedar wood was burning faintly in the corner. Closing her eyes, she inhaled the relaxing scent deep into her lungs, her stare faltering briefly onto scattered sheets of parchment on his bed, a quill sat deep in ink.

He had been writing letters again, every year without fail, to lay by his parents' graves, and she realised today was not the best day for bad news. But he hadn't said anything. Instead, he shuffled the pages together into a bundle and set them aside within the confines of the bedside drawer.

She redirected her focus, sitting down on the floor, legs crossed, reaching out with her palms, allowing the emanating warmth to almost burn her fingers. The dancing flames started to relax her frozen bones and she wiggled them, then curled them into fists. Repeating the motion several times before she found the strength to speak. Wind howled through the cracked glass from a small window by the low ceiling. Then, poison seeped onto her tongue when she answered, "The other side of the Crossroads."

"The bodies?"

"Burned."

There was no urgency in his voice, just a low, noncommittal murmur. "Nothing new."

The way the whole house burned down to smoldering coals flashed before her eyes as if she was still there, walking through remnants, kicking planks of wood aside that crackled with a faint, dying flame. Ashes tasted too strong on her tongue, clambering into her nostrils in disgusting, hard-to-breathe wafts.

"But that doesn't explain why you've come here while they're practically next door." Oliver moved the animal skins on his bed, heaving himself onto the straw filled mattress and slumping his back against the wall. "I was coming to see you tomorrow."

She rubbed her eyes, staring into the flame of the candle and said reassuringly, "It'll be fine."

"What if they knock on my door to check if I'm harbouring a criminal?"

"Is that what we're called now? Criminals?" She shook her head. "There isn't a way to tell me apart."

"There is. Haven't you heard?"

Her head perked up and she fixed her eyes on him for the first time that night, her reddened cheeks thawing. She swept the damp chestnut curls from her forehead. "Heard what?"

He explained calmly, "Isla has her hands on a potion. It's supposed to reveal if you're Drishti by changing your eye colour back for a split second. The way it changes when you're trying to control someone."

Concern skimmed Ezme's features as her brows furrowed, but soon she relaxed and sighed. "Just another danger to hide from." With a low creak in her voice that made it falter, she repeated more to herself than to him, "It'll be fine."

There was so much to discuss but she couldn't bring herself to begin. It was too late, and her eyes felt heavy along with the energy seeping away from her shoulders.

She let him take her hand and pull her up from the floor towards a spot next to him. She lay down, resting her head against a feather pillow, sewn patterns of blue petalled flowers splayed whimsically in disarray. The sleeves of her oversized jumper were still damp with an underlying tone of a burnt smell.

Rows of candles made Oliver's small house feel like home, the fragrance lingering. Although the sight of a small leather-bound flask filled with, what she suspected, a poisonous brew in the half-open drawer, mere inches below the tabletop, sent a chill through her body. With the amounts of deaths they had been witnessing, she wasn't surprised when Oliver didn't react to the news the way she hoped; with shock or disgust or even an underlying hatred, but rather with poignant stoicism.

There was a chest of drawers next to the bed where his bag was tossed aside, and in the gap between the flap she could see rolls of bandages sticking out. The straps of the bag had stains of blood, probably imprinted by Oliver's quick hands, as he grabbed a fresh bandage from his bag when tending to others' injuries. Recently, he had his hands full as a healer.

"If it'll make you feel better, we can send Blade to check on Esteracre and your father," he whispered, cuddling her from behind as she shuffled closer to his chest, redirecting her attention away from the bloody bag.

Despite her best attempts to hide her worried breath, he knew her well enough to understand she wasn't scared for herself, never had been. She was worried about everyone else.

He added, "And as soon as the sun rises, we can move to Lorkeep to make sure everything is in order as it should be. If Valeis guards moved south through the town of Blackwick to the Crossroads, Lorkeep might be the next target. We need to warn them of the possibility."

His warm and gentle voice resonated in her ear, soothing her worries away, if only for a moment. She nodded, sighing quietly as Oliver covered their feet up to their necks with a dirtied woollen blanket. He turned to face the wall while Ezme brought her knees up to her chest, their backs almost touching. She felt safe despite the gap between them, letting her eyes rest.

She thought of the time she had last seen Blade. It was two whole winters ago, right before her seventeenth birthday – on the very day she wished to forget. That night, although Ezme hated to admit it, she had been glad Blade was there. Their gaze met only for a moment, but long enough for Ezme to understand that Blade wasn't going to let Oliver get hurt, before she turned away and left. After all, he was her only friend.

Everyone knew exactly what Blade was capable of, and that a knife in her hand was as deadly as a dose of poison.

CHAPTER 2

For everyone at the market the scent of fresh bread made their mouths water, except for Blade's. She'd already eaten, stuffing the remaining bit of pungent cheese back into some ruffled brown paper and into the side of her pocket. She wiped her blade clean from slicing away the natural layer of mold and tossed it for the birds to feed on.

The wheeled carriages and stalls were overwhelmed with villagers, coughing up dirt every time they were transported. Spices, venison meat and the smell of fish brought down from the harbour tickled her nose. Steps quickened.

She hated to be amongst vast amounts of people with an uncontained passion, but her shoes could not withstand any more mice nibbling in that forsaken hut she lived in, forcing her to venture out further than she planned to in order to find a pair that would fit her.

She stopped before a mirror to see gently flowing, warm hues of burnt strands reach her lower back; a shade that leaned brown yet embraced the naturally rusty, flaming auburn. Her hand reached up to ruffle the hair on her forehead and to fix a piece of narrow, clotted fabric across the top of her head, tied behind her ears like a headband. Her reflection caught the depths of her almond-shaped, blue eyes containing just a hint of a daring sparkle and her small lips were deeply defined with a cupid's bow. She realised her cheek was smeared with something black, probably coal from trying to warm up her chimney last night, so she spat on her sleeve and wiped it off.

"Watch where you're going!" she gasped, exhaling and rolling her eyes at a young lad rolling a heavy barrel across the dusty path which almost crashed into her. She managed to avoid it at the last second.

She heard him stammer an apology after her, hurrying across to set the barrel beside one of the stalls surrounded with casks of ale and spiced mead, but she ignored him, listening to the sound of a hammer nearby. Behind one of the carriages, a cobbler worked on a pair of boots a few sizes too big for her, sweat dripping from his forehead.

Sneaking in with the crowd, she slipped around the cobbler's stall and into his carriage. Her hands rummaged quickly through crates of newly made shoes, however, none of them matched her small-sized feet. With a glance at repaired shoes, she heaved a sigh, eventually deciding to grab a pair of leather boots that belonged to somebody else, leaving her own battered pair behind in an attempt at an honest exchange.

She peeked out behind the carriage's grey curtain, ripped and patched up many times over. When the coast was clear, she jumped off the ledge, disappearing into another wave of villagers. They all seemed to be hustling in an over-excited rush to a brand-new stall she'd never seen before, filled with colourful thin vials and flasks of claimed magical elixirs. She snorted at their stupidity, knowing there was no such thing.

"Blade!"

She turned on the tips of her toes, testing the balance of her new shoes. Her hand hovered just above her hip. Recognising the thick brown hair moving in her direction, she lowered her hand, relaxing her muscles.

"What do you want?" Behind Oliver, her eyes focused on Ezme. "You bring all your late-night companions to tend to business?"

Oliver ignored the remark. "I'm not on my way to tend to any business. We need your help."

"Sounds like business to me." She crossed her arms, waiting, but when Ezme opened her mouth to speak, she snapped, "She doesn't speak."

Ezme let out an irritated breath, stepping away from them, pretending to be interested in hand-made ornaments within a huge wheelbarrow, picking one and turning it in her fingers, allowing the seller to ramble on about his products.

Oliver kept his tone low, standing inches from Blade now. "Isla killed last night, and we're headed to Lorkeep to warn them. I need someone to send word to Esteracre."

"Let me guess…You want *me* to go to Esteracre, not *someone*." She tiptoed to look over his shoulder, scanning the surroundings quickly. "To be absolutely honest with you, this particular task wasn't on my list of things to do today so I think my answer will be *no* to that."

"Ten coins?"

"Ten? I have better things to attend to," she snarled, turning away.

Oliver grabbed her wrist, bringing her closer, forcing her head to inch upward to look into his darkening green eyes. "Children are at risk. Twenty coins is my final offer and I hope one day you'll learn to care about something other than just yourself."

She snatched her hand away from him, a chuckle playing on her lips when she said, "Now, that's something I'm inclined to consider."

Ezme rushed over to them. "Is that..." The question died on her lips and she gulped down a worried sob threatening to escape. Their heads immediately followed the direction of her pointed finger.

Nobody around them paid any attention. Blade shuffled on the spot, tiptoeing to see above peoples' heads in front. In the distance, above a clamour of trees, they saw a faint trickle of foggy smoke. Almost invisible to those who weren't looking for it, but undeniably present.

Blade was aware of four hidden locations to keep Drishti children safe. Four locations that she herself knew. There were others, but if she hadn't stumbled upon them, it meant they were well protected, even for her. From what Oliver explained, the Crossroads' safe place burned down, leaving nothing but ashes, and now Lorkeep's shelter was on fire as they stood there, watching in an uncomfortable squirm.

It took one look at Oliver for Blade to nod sharply and rush through the crowd, pushing people aside to make it to the edge of the woods, mounting a horse and subsequently leaving Ezme and Oliver far behind.

With skilful fingers, she tied a rope around a tree a few paces before the shelter, leaving her mare concealed behind a shrub and low hanging branches. With her hands pressed against the bark of a birch tree, she peered behind it, then dared stepping into the open plateau, heaving her weight against the heavy door to force her way into the shelter. She scanned the room, covering her mouth with the sleeve of her slim-fitted coat, listening for even the barest of noises. All she heard was a crackling fire coming from one end and spreading fast across the wooden floor devouring everything on its way.

She could tell there was something above, as the house from outside appeared much taller and there were no stairs inside to investigate further; just a soot-stained ceiling, soon to collapse.

She retracted her steps, manoeuvring over blackened furniture, stepping out of the house. Water welled up in her eyes as she let out a dry cough. She circled the house, finding another door leading to the attic up the crooked stairs, nestled with sprouting, wayward weeds. The door hung off its hinges and she heard a voice, loud and clear, "As soon as you get down, I'll give the likes of you a swift end, wretched child."

The soldier's voice huffed below a little boy curled above the wooden beams close to the ceiling. He clung with both of his small arms to the highest beam he could reach. The Valeis guard kept reaching for him, nearing closer with his grubby hands.

Blade's hand instinctively grasped a small dagger from the sheath by her black belt, turning it in between her fingers only once. The soldier managed to pull the boy's leg down and that's when Blade threw her knife into his back. He staggered backward and fell on one knee. She walked up to him, withdrew the blade and, with a smooth motion, sliced his throat. Blood trickled from his mouth as she nudged him forward. He fell with a thud, causing dust to rise around his motionless body.

She set the dagger back into its sheath and wiped her bloodied hand on the back of the guard's combat trousers. There was no way she was going to ruin her newly acquired pair with easy blood. Her eyes shifted to the boy who was still clutching onto the beam with tears on his cheeks.

She extended a hand. "Come now, I won't hurt you."

The boy hesitated, gaping at the dead man below with an open mouth, then forced himself to clamp it shut, swallowing a shaky breath.

"Come now, otherwise we'll both burn to death or fall through the floor and the whole saving you thing will be for absolutely nothing."

He pursed his lips, nonetheless, slid down into her arms and remained behind her until they reached open-air. Ezme and Oliver arrived at the same time. Their breaths were out of place. Ezme clasped her hands above her kneecaps, resting and engulfing fresh air into her lungs. Her cheeks were painted a splash of pink and her eyes were full of horror, staring out of a soft, round face, as they searched around for missing people.

"Where are the rest of…"

The little boy pointed towards a shed behind them. Mercilessly burned. The black flames charred the walls whole and the flimsy roof collapsed into ashes. However, the house still burned with flames so fierce they matched Blade's hair. Dancing on every last bit of furniture, licking angrily at the remains of the walls.

They stood there. Simply watching.

Oliver crouched down by the boy, bringing his bag in front by his feet. "Are you hurt?" he asked.

The boy extended his arm to show a cut above his elbow. Oliver gently rolled the sleeve of the top up, holding his hand in his. With the other, he fetched a small bottle of spirit from his bag.

"This is going to itch for a moment, but I want to clean your wound to make sure an infection won't fester. Is that okay?"

The boy pressed his lips together, knitting his eyebrows in anticipation when Oliver unscrewed the cap and poured a small amount of the clear liquid onto the cut. The boy's arm jerked, but he bravely held his breath, squirming and waiting for the burning sensation to pass.

Ezme's hand was twitching by her side as she tried to focus and bring her attention to the boy. "What's your name?"

"A–Adie," he managed, biting hard on his lip. The tears on his cheeks were dried up with fresh ones welling in the hollows of his eyes. His face blackened with smoke.

She turned to Oliver, "We have to take him to Esteracre right away and hope they haven't been found yet."

Oliver managed to tie a dressing around Adie's arm before the boy pulled away, looking at Ezme sceptically. "I don't want to…You can't take me anywhere."

Adie clung to Blade's leg, stomping his foot, and she had an overcoming urge to brush him away. Instead, she gritted her teeth and crouched down next to his trembling body. "Listen, kid."

He furrowed his eyebrows at her, letting his posture uncurl, suddenly seeming a few inches taller. His face was dark, but his eyes were a strong gloom of grey. "I'm eleven."

"Kid," she repeated, "it's just another day where you're not sheltered in a warm home, but in the real world; in the world where you'll learn that people die. It happens all the time. All your friends are dead. Do you want to die next or do you want to try to live another day like the rest of us here?"

Ezme scoffed, "For heaven's sake, Blade! Is that how you talk to a child?"

Blade straightened up, resting her gaze on Oliver. "I guess my work here is done since you're heading to

Esteracre yourselves." She extended her upturned palm towards him. "I seem to have helped. I'll collect what's mine now."

She disappeared into the woods, throwing a jingling satchel up and down in one hand.

CHAPTER 3

Gusts of bitter wind seeped into the chinks in the walls and shelter was limited to Blackwick villagers outside the castle gate. Richer families closed their doors tight and spent their days curled up in sheep skins around a fireplace, burning chunks of wood down to ashes all night long. Poorer families, however, sought warmth by huddling next to each other through those never-ending evenings, seeking rays of sun on their faces and frozen bones in the mornings. To enjoy winter was to possess adequate resources to survive its unforgiving reign.

For the first time in a long time, December hadn't seen a coat of snow atop the roofs or any of the paths surrounding the castle grounds. Instead of a joyous winter, grey skies and the bleak possibility of a white flutter made everyone irritable.

The afternoon on the castle grounds was no different; children played with scarves wrapped around their necks and thick leather gloves warming up their brittle bones. But one boy had his gloves off, trampled by his feet, flimsy fingers stuffing something into his coat.

"No! Stop! He's my friend!" Cassandra screamed, running towards a guard who had his sword extended to the boy's chest. "I order you to stop right this second!"

The guard held the sword firmly pointed, his eyes squarely on the boy, unwavering.

"Let him go or my mother will find out about this," she hissed, her lips pursing. She curled her fingers into fists, her nails digging into her palms.

"Now, now, sweetheart," a sweet voice came from behind Cassandra and she turned sharply, her eyes pleading for the boy's life. "Who is your father, boy?" she addressed him. The guard lowered the sword and held it tightly by his side, awaiting instruction, and slightly bowing his head to the Queen.

The boy stammered, "My–my father is a sword–swordsmith. He–he made this one."

He jutted his chin at the sword that only moments ago scratched his chest. He recognised the fine edge finish of the blade and the engraved pommel forming the shape of three pointy flames – the symbol of the land of Valeis.

"Very well, swordsmith's spawn," the Queen muttered. As she turned, she instructed her guard, "A beating will teach him a lesson more valuable than death. For now."

"Mother, you can't…I told him to steal that pie from the merch! It was me who told him…"

The Queen measured her breaths and the number of steps it took her to stand beside Cassandra, her tall figure loomed over the girl and her lips turned into a nasty snarl. "You will never lie again."

Cassandra's pale cheeks flushed crimson, and a tear threatened to fall. Her lower lip wobbled, but she bit it hard, then turned away from the boy and walked behind her mother, overhearing painful yelps all the way to the entrance of the palace where they finally quietened, dispersing against the walls.

Queen Isla stopped in her tracks, casting a slow glance around the tapestries until her beady eyes fell squarely on her daughter's. She commanded, "Princesses don't cry."

"Princesses don't cry," Cassandra uttered the words her mother spoke a few years ago, picking a comb up from the silver-plated dresser, brushing through her long, golden locks. The mirror hanging on the wall was so huge she could easily count the freckles on her nose.

"I'm glad you've finally learned the lesson. I only mean what's good for you, dear."

The door to Princess Cassandra's chambers flew open and the Queen's personal guard stepped in, bowing his head low, never meeting their gaze. A small golden Valeis pommel shone on the left side of his chest, darkening the closer he stood. "Queen Isla."

"Speak," she responded curtly.

"Drishti men have been lined up for your pick."

"Very well. Wait outside."

With a last long look in the mirror, Cassandra inhaled deeply, holding her breath for a moment before releasing it, and with a steady hand setting the comb back down.

With a velvet hood over her head, all she could focus on were Queen Isla's heavy footsteps sounding through the murky corridors until they reached the grounds and a warm ray of sun hit her face. She released a single button of her cloak, its hem skimming the stone path behind her. The sleeves looped by her wrists as she extended her hand to adjust a silver feather necklace, turning it face-out and letting it tumble down her cleavage. A soft, light blue dress hugged around her slim figure, falling gently to her ankles. The fresh breeze pinched her cheeks and her freckles appeared more prominent.

Iron-wrought gates hurled open and she followed the stairs down, becoming darker and darker, illuminated only by fire torches on brick walls. It was dead silent except for coughs and sniffles coming from one of the men standing in line.

"Make your choice, dear," Queen Isla prompted, stepping aside into a shadow. Her presence pierced the air with sharp arrows, making the dungeons feel smaller than they were.

Cassandra gulped down. Come spring she was to turn eighteen and that meant coronation day. Queen Isla was to step down to welcome Cassandra as the new Queen. But the winter was long, and Cassandra wished for it to hurry and thaw away the bitter coldness.

One of the men in line, Cree, looked pale with a terrible fever written all over his face in a sickly grey undertone. His lips were dry, cracked. He wouldn't last a week without medicine. He held himself up, hand over his stomach, hollows for eyes, deep ridges forming beneath.

She cleared her throat and cursed herself to say the wrong words. She could hear Isla's words echoing in the depths of her mind urging her to not make a mistake.

A strong man to stand next to you…

A man who'd make you powerful and fierce…

Most importantly, his duty is to give you a Drishti heir to the throne…

"I shall marry whomever you deem suitable, Mother," she responded. Her voice was flat with no emotion. Deep down, she knew this was the only right answer to give.

She fought against the crumbling sensation – the selfish desire to show her hand, but she withheld her own opinion. All that was expected from her was to uphold the pure Drishti rule with a man that was a pure Drishti suitor. Accustomed to the castle. Accustomed to everything they lived by.

Whomever her mother was going to choose, she would make it work. She had to. She had a rough idea of who it was going to be. She refrained from looking his way, but she could feel his stare on her, judging her with the same eyes she saw through those bars on occasional visits to the dungeons. They were always filled with a sense of sorrow and regret she couldn't quite understand.

Cassandra bit down on her tongue, stopping herself from saying more than she should. Casting her eyes to the side, away from the men behind the bars, she caught a glimpse of a sly smile welcoming one corner of Isla's mouth. The shadows cast from the fire torches upon Isla's milk white skin accentuated her sharply slanted cheekbones and slender neckline. In old paintings, she had an ethereal quality about her, a glowing look that Cassandra imagined held everyone's stares. Now, the fragility of her delicate beauty was gone, replaced by rough edges and sharp lines.

CHAPTER 4

"Since you were born, our cabin has never been compromised. We'll carry on as we are. Under Isla's control, Valeis guards killed before and no doubt will again," Victor announced to Ezme, gulping down a keg of beer. He wiped the foam from his moustache, setting down the remnants of the beverage heavy on the table.

"Ezme," Victor grunted, tapping his large fingers on the table, trying to reassure her, "the children are safe with us."

She took a moment to ponder, then said, "We've been lucky so far." The herbal beverage lodged tightly between her hands felt cold, having held it for a long time without taking a single sip from it. "But luck eventually runs out. I want to make sure we do everything to keep—"

"We've kept *you* protected. We'll do the same for the children that took your place here," Victor cut in, the edge of his voice sharp and his expression hardened.

Ezme opened her mouth, then clamped it shut, meeting his eyes for a brief moment. She dipped her head in agreement, nudging her mug away to the middle of the table.

Victor was a scrubby man in his late forties with broad shoulders, his longer hair tied back into a clean bun. He scratched his beard before propelling himself up and pushing the chair backward, the legs squealing against the floor. His calloused hands picked up a rusty axe and he left through the door, dragging his feet into the Esteracre woods, following the direction of the afternoon sun.

Ezme laid her elbows on the table, burying her face into open palms. The thick, long curls spilled over the edge in unruly spirals, suspended in the air.

The children at Esteracre had a strict etiquette to follow. They were not allowed out during the hours of the day, restricting their evening activities to a minimum, under close supervision by either Richard, Ezme's father, or Victor, his friend. That way, even if Valeis guards marched through Esteracre woods discovering their location, the children would be safe within the confines of the walls.

When Ezme was young, a hidden bunker had been built to ensure that if danger presented itself, they would all have an outlet to stay safe. She had to hide there only once before – the memory of it tasted bitter on her tongue.

As she pushed herself off from the table, shoving the chair under the wooden top, sharp, metallic grey eyes stared at her. A pair of arms embraced her thighs, locking small fingers together at the back, digging a high ponytail against her stomach.

"Emilia."

Ezme instantly smiled, patting the top of the girl's head. Crouching down to pull Emilia into her arms, she lifted her up on the side of her hip.

"Will you come with me?" the girl asked, planting a kiss on Ezme's cheek.

Ezme knew the answer, but asked anyway, "Where are we going?"

"To the super-secret hideout!"

"Again?" Ezme laughed. "We have a small mission today. We have to show Adie what we do in an emergency. Would you like to help?"

Emilia nodded, her feet kicking excitedly in the air. She could hardly contain the massive smile since laying her eyes on Ezme. It had only been two days, but to the little girl, probably felt like an eternity.

"Adie!" Emilia shouted, baring a hole into the door with her eyes, impatiently waiting for him to enter the room.

Adie appeared beside them, reluctantly dragging his feet across the floor with a questioning expression. Ezme shifted Emilia higher on her hip; she wasn't getting any smaller and to carry her around was slowly becoming burdensome. Oliver was better fitted for this job, Ezme thought, strengthening her hold.

"This is Emilia," Ezme introduced them at which point Adie shrugged. "You'll have to listen carefully to what I'm going to tell you. For your own safety and everybody else's – in case Valeis guards were to march anywhere near this cabin. There are a few rules to follow and this is the most important one of them all. Understood?"

His shoulders shrugged again in a noncommittal manner and he fidgeted with his hands in front.

The passage to the bunker was under one of the furry sheepskin rugs. Emilia didn't like its smell, washing her hands fervently under cold water every time she touched it, but she pulled it off, tugging it to the side. The entry hatch was hardly visible; the lines cleverly intertwined along the floor panels. With her fingers, she slipped them down a small crevice that looked like a sliver of wood had cracked away, lifting it smoothly open and revealing a set of dim ladders below.

Ezme found herself in the gloomy chamber, hands searching through dust and cobwebs for a pack of matches to light the thin, white candle. Its wick turned black in an instant. The oil lanterns were stored in a dust-covered crate, one on top of the other, lined up against the wall in a row. They were designed to give warmth and feeble visibility for a very long time.

Adie pulled a face but his feet, nonetheless, followed Emilia as she dragged him forward by the hem of his sleeve showing him around. There wasn't much to show. Empty stone walls, irregular in their form, didn't hold warmth, making the air damp and murky. If it wasn't for the candlelight, everything would be pitch-black. An arch led to a smaller space; cushions spread across the ground covering every inch. The biggest hide belonged to a brown bear laid out flat below multiples of calf skins, goatskins and deerskins.

"We're supposed to come here right away if we see any of the guards," Emilia stated, laying down on the skins, spreading her arms like a snow angel.

"Victor, as the only commoner amongst us, will cover the hatch with the rug, allowing the guards to search through if they so wished. They wouldn't find us. The hatch locks from the inside with a series of key chained padlocks to prevent them from opening it up from outside.

"All we have to do is get here and lock it. And most important of all – keep absolutely quiet. Not a peep. Like a mouse under a rug."

"We are under a rug!" Emilia giggled, rocking up from her back onto crossed legs.

Ezme continued, "They'd have no reason to suspect there was anything below deck if only we keep absolutely quiet."

"And if things don't go according to plan?" Adie asked sceptically.

Ezme waved Emilia over, helping her climb the ladder back up. Then, she wet her fingers to extinguish the flame on the candle, laying it flat beside the bottom of the metal rods. As she did that, she told Adie, letting him go in front of her, "Let's hope they do."

From outside the house, below the drain, Oliver grabbed a bucket full of rainwater from the night before and poured it into a pot hung above a fire stove. Ezme fiddled with a pack of matches, letting the wood catch flame. She flicked a loose strand of hair behind her ear as thoughts curled in her mind, enjoying the smell of the burnt matchstick.

Children's voices resonated through the walls. The door to their room was half-open, allowing both Ezme and Oliver to glimpse at them from time to time. Adie twiddled with his hands, sitting beside Quinto who was reading an illustrated book on his bed. Ember was trying to assemble a bird feeder to hang outside on one of the bigger trees while Emilia, Liya and Khari sat in a circle on the floor, telling each other stories.

Adie didn't look their way, but he heard the aim of the game was to catch someone in a lie. To his understanding, all of the stories they've told each other were lies, made up and not real. He didn't see the point of it.

As Victor was chopping wood on a stump beside the house, the oldest of the children, Beckett, sneaked out through the back door to catch an unsuspecting toad in his bare hands. Seeing him, Ezme smiled to herself, shaking her head. Victor heard a hushed voice while drawing the axe down, splitting a chunk of wood in half in one hit.

He said to himself, clear and loud enough for Beckett to hear, "If I turn around and see any of you outside…"

Beckett scooted back inside, stuffing the slimy toad into one of his pockets. The moment he had entered the room, the circle of lies diffused and almost everyone joined in on passing the trilling toad from hand to hand, laughing and pulling faces at each other. Almost everyone joined in, except for Emilia who stood in the corner screwing her face at their mucky hands and Adie who remained in his seat, observing them cautiously.

"I've cut up all the carrots," Oliver proclaimed, laying the knife down on the tabletop. He gathered all the compost in a bowl and threw it outside for the night animals to ruffle through.

"I'm a little worried about Adie," Ezme said when Oliver returned to the kitchen.

She dropped a whole skinned chicken in the boiling water, bubbles rippling on the surface, before adding wedges of potatoes with skin, thinly chopped onions, neat talons of carrots she'd waited a long time for, and a bunch of celery sticks.

"Give him some time. It's normal to stray away in a new environment. He's just testing the waters before jumping with both feet."

She sprinkled thyme and bay leaves, then salt and peppercorns, stirring the contents with a wooden spoon.

"I'd like to believe you're right," she muttered, watching as the ingredients whirled in the boiling water.

The soup was poured into plates and bowls. Victor took a seat at the top of the long, wooden table he had crafted himself, the edges filed down into a smooth finish. One end had a wonky leg and wobbled slightly every time the weight shifted. Handfuls of bread were dipped in the soup. Victor occasionally grunted and lifted his eyes from over his own plate every time any of the children spread their elbows wide atop the table, or when Beckett threw wet bay leaves at the girls across from him.

Ezme pinched a slice of bread from a wicker basket and took the opportunity to sit alone on the front porch step, picking tremulously at the hard sourdough crust with her fingers. The world had gone silent around her as she stared into the surrounding treetops for what seemed like an eternity, enjoying the sounds of hums from inside and the clatter of cutlery.

The cabin was engulfed within the canopy of Esteracre woods. There were no trails leading to it, except for a thin barren path from the front door to a trickling mountain stream where Victor brought buckets of water from each morning.

The crumbs fell on Ezme's knees, attracting white bellied sparrows with their heads twisting up, sneaking up closer and closer until finally, she tossed the last bit of bread for them to nibble on. She fidgeted with the ends of her hair, tediously winding and unwinding them around a finger in contemplation. She shifted, blinking excessively, when a hand waved inches away from her nose.

"Are you there?" asked Oliver, bemused.

"Sorry," she muttered, gave her head a shake and looked down at her nails. They were dirty and she began scratching at them.

He took a seat next to her. "Not eating?"

"Victor told me as soon as my father heard about the Crossroads fire, he ventured out to check on Zeffari's Keep. If all is well, I suspect he'll be back by morning."

"Then morning we shall await," he responded, grinning, playfully nudging her with his shoulder, attempting to spark a sly smile that tugged hidden at her lips. "Let's go for a walk."

Her forehead creased. "What about your dinner?"

"Dinner can wait, but the sun might not."

She took his hand and followed him into the woods. Silence hung in the thick air as they set off along a channel of water with a gentle slope. They jumped across the stream, careful not to slip on the wet stones and fall in. The sound of a screeching eagle, somewhere far, broke the silence as the sun began to descend to meet the horizon.

"Just like old times?" he asked when they reached an obelisk where dark-green wintergreens climbed on top of each other along its walls. Ezme ran her hand through their rough leaves, remembering how their colour shone brighter last time they came here, now shadowed by high trees.

Oliver ambled cautiously behind her as she propelled herself up, sliding the tips of her shoes inside a chink in the stone. They sat on the rock, watching the sun disappear until a chill made Ezme shiver. Oliver put his arm around her, bringing her head under his chin.

"Last time we sat on this rock, I might have liked you a little bit more than was expected," she blurted out before she could bite her tongue.

"Expected? Is there a rule for liking someone a little bit more that I'm not aware of?" he mused, laughing.

She hesitated, looking out above the treetops in an absent gaze until his laugh quietened. "Can I tell you something?"

"Always."

"Promise not to laugh at me."

"I guess I'll try not to," he said. "But I can't exactly promise—"

She sputtered out a confession that had been curling in her mind for some time, "I wanted to kiss you back then, but I ended up biting my tongue and not saying a word about it since."

"Why not?"

She shook her head, suddenly noticing how heavy his arm felt around her. She wasn't sure why she would have mentioned it in the first place. "I didn't think you would like me…at least in that way, so it was easier not to say anything." She pulled away from him. "I think it was for the best anyway."

He cleared his throat, running his hand through his hair. "I guess when you spend so much time together, you sometimes get stupid ideas."

She shoved him aside, pulling her legs up to her chest, entangling her arms around them. He dropped his shoulders and clasped his hands together in his lap.

"Have you ever wondered how it would feel?" he asked, but his voice quivered, unsure if he wanted to hear the answer.

Some things were always best left unsaid.

"We've…" She instinctively bit her tongue. "I don't know if thinking about it is a good idea. We've been friends forever. I don't even know why I would bring this up. It was ages ago since we last sat here. I just remembered it," she muttered, smiling to herself. "Places bring back memories, you know?"

He dropped his head briefly, staring at his hands, then looked back up to meet her gaze. "And what about now? How do you feel about it now?"

A pang in the pit of Ezme's stomach rooted her down. Slowly, he leaned in and her heart lodged in her throat. She felt his measured and steady breath on her cheek, and she dipped her head sideways, gathering her thoughts.

"Oli—"

"Ez, one kiss won't hurt," he murmured, his voice a hint deeper than usual, his lips almost brushing against her ear, sending shivers down her spine.

She lifted her chin up to look at him. Words failed her as he moved closer.

A few inches away.

Everything inside her floated dangerously, despite trying to stay calm on the outside. He felt her breath shorten and fasten; her eyes unable to fix onto anything except his slightly parted lips ending in a diminutive curve.

An inch away.

Less than an inch.

His lips found their way against hers.

Soft. Moving like they belonged there. She forgot where she was. He cupped her chin with one hand and she immediately grabbed onto it with both of hers, leaning in closer, wanting his lips never to leave hers, but he parted, taking a rugged breath.

She dropped her hands onto her lap, observing how his chest rose and fell out of pace and the way his teeth bore into his lower lip in a crooked, charming smile.

He pressed his palms down on the rock, picking himself up, then offered her a hand. "We should get going."

The walk back was quiet and Ezme's thoughts were filled with so many questions she didn't want to ask – questions she equally wanted to know the answers to – and her insides still veered. She focused on how the leaves on the ground crunched underneath her shoes, suddenly aware of how unnaturally loud she was breathing.

The glimmer of her heart peaked upward when she felt his hand slide into hers. An unspoken promise. Reassurance she needed.

As they stepped through the door, the children were already in bed. Six wooden beds with wool blankets and a freshly made cedar wood plank for Adie that Victor had finished before dinner was served.

Oliver turned to Ezme after making sure the door was locked and secured with multiple locks. "I'll see you in the morning," he whispered, giving her a subtle peck on the top of her head, then set off to rest on the sofa.

She opened up a cabinet by the staircase and drew out a blanket, throwing it to him. "Keep warm, Oli."

Taking the stairs up, she slipped through the door to her bedroom, finding comfort under the covers, staring out the window at the stars before her eyelids gave way and sleep caught up with her muddled thoughts.

CHAPTER 5

Adie tossed and turned during his first night at the Esteracre cabin. His gloomy grey eyes could almost reflect the moon as he stared at it beneath an obscure window, its curtains drawn open. His linen night tunic was dripping in sweat. He let the animal hide covering his chest fall between the wall and bed. Blurred wisps of dark shadows formed in front of his eyes.

In the depths of his imagination, he felt someone walk up to him and dig their nails into his shin, dragging him off the bed and into the unknown. The simple thought of fire, burning hot and devouring everything in its way, prickled his skin. He pulled his knees up to his chest, encircling them with shaking arms.

He felt like he didn't belong. He had lost all of his friends, the people who took care of him. More than anything in the world, he wished to be back with his parents, before they gave him up, knowing what sort of life awaited him. There were a few things he knew before he was ordered to leave his home. He was Drishti and that was reason enough to tear a child away from their mother. The lasting image that was stuck at the back of his mind was the hardened lines forming his mother's lips.

Run, Adie. Run as fast as you can.

Don't turn back. Please, Adie. You need to listen.

He didn't want to go anywhere. This was his home.

We don't want you here.

The words sunk into his chest like an anchor in a frail attempt to protect him. His grey eyes glinted in a puddle when he tripped, the night crickets and low growls angling around him, slashing his palms in riveting red pools on the harsh gravel. He wept, his hands were blackened with smears and so were his cheeks as he tried to wipe away the tears that would not stop falling.

Adie shook his head, stopping the dangerous shadows from closing in on him, laying amongst slow whistles of sleeping children around him. Nature started to wake up with a low chirping of birds outside.

He sneaked around the wooden beds. Not one of the children stirred, as he tiptoed to the door. He passed Oliver, who clambered on the sofa in an uncomfortable position, the covers hanging from his foot to the floor. Adie unlocked the door, pulling the rusty chain back with a quiet rattle. With one last look at Oliver, he found himself outside, willing his feet to lead him somewhere else. A place where he wasn't just another child that needed protecting from the world.

He walked on and on until he'd stumbled upon three men. An older man with a dirtied coat, sleeves longer than his arms, thick, unruly hair, that hadn't seen a comb in a long time, and a beard frosted with grey specks. Two Valeis guards accompanied him – one of them shorter by a whole head than the other, swords with scabbards at their belts, dressed in a dark brown shade of fitted uniform.

"State your business in these woods," the taller of the Valeis guards ordered, stopping the older man, before realising there was a wolf lurking just behind a tree, observing them with its ears pointed upward.

The shorter guard shifted his weight from one leg to the other as the wolf bared his teeth, reaching the older man's leg. The man caressed the side of the wolf's furry jaw, pointing a finger down to the ground for him to sit. The wolf obeyed.

The man managed a faint smile. "Just going home. I like to take early morning strolls. It's beautiful here. Just wherever the winds take me really."

The guards exchanged a glance. The shorter of the two had small beads of sweat trickling down from his brow now. He pursed his lips.

The taller guard continued, "Where is home for you?"

The vein on the older man's neck throbbed under his collar and the button threatened to suffocate him. The guard's expression remained set, tapping his long fingernails against the hilt of the weapon.

The wolf pounced on all fours when his master replied, "Oh – just near the Crossroads."

"That's quite a long stroll all the way into the midst of Esteracre woods. Isn't it?"

The shorter guard nodded, looping his fingers on each side of the belt, his eyes never straying away from the furry companion.

"Sir, we won't bother you anymore." The guard's face relaxed and he reached into his coat. "Just drink this and we'll be on our way."

It was a small vial with coils of colours mixing in and out.

A potion to expose Drishti.

The options narrowed down. He was too old and too slow to run away from them. A tail snaked around his bare ankle, giving him an ounce of confidence to take the vial into his hand, forcing it to remain unshaken. The sharpened knife on the inside of his waistcoat suddenly felt heavy, rubbing against his ribs.

The moment he reached for it, the wolf, as if on command, pounced at the shorter man's leg. His teeth sunk deep. Blood oozed onto bleak yellow leaves beneath.

As soon as the handle of the knife cooled his enclosed palm, the taller guard pulled a sturdy, slick dagger from the back of his belt. Without a moment's hesitation, he dragged it through the man's stomach, pushing as far as it would go, then pulling it out and cleaning the blade with the man's sleeve, jolting him upright against a tree.

The wolf quavered and released his grip on the leg when the taller guard unsheathed his glistening sword, slashing it down into the ground where the wolf was a mere second ago. With a growl, he backed up, still looking at the older man, his tail retracting in between his legs and one ear folding over.

"Go…" the older man gargled, his words a shocked whisper.

"It's like they want to get killed," the taller guard snorted as he helped the shorter limp away, leaving the older man to bleed out. "Wandering out in the open like this."

Adie's eyes bulged out, scanning around for anything that would help. The man clutched the wound with both hands, sliding down against the tree bark with his back, a deep rumble of pain in his throat.

Adie ran. Back to the cabin as fast as he could, scratching his hands on the hard leaves, batting them away from his face, stinging nettle brushing against his ankles. He panted, pushing the door wide open, so far it slammed against the wall. Small hands shook Oliver awake.

"You have to help me. There's a man. In the forest. Dying. Hurry!"

Oliver stirred and before he knew, bolted out the door with Adie leading the way. Negative thoughts kept crawling into Oliver's mind, no matter how many times he willed them away. He had to hurry his steps, but he could only go as fast as Adie. The boy, although trying his best, found himself stumbling over rocks every now and then.

"Richard!" Oliver yelled as he neared the man, taking off his own coat and thin jumper.

He pulled it around the bleeding stomach, tightening it, slipping the coat over Richard's arms to keep his body temperature warm. Oliver noticed a single sun ray bouncing off a glass vial, sticking out of tall grass. He returned his attention back to Richard, heaving him onto his feet and propelling his body weight onto his shoulders.

Richard grunted, "Tell Ez—"

"We're close to home," Oliver huffed, interrupting him, "we'll get you there. Adie, help me out here!"

Adie was standing metres away, clutching his arms around a young tree, half looking and half scanning the woods, his lips trembling in shock. Bravely, he tried to assist from the other side, feeling Richard's heavy hand crush his shoulder down. He pursed his lips, using the last ounce of strength his small body could muster in getting Richard back.

They lowered Richard down on the couch inside the cabin while all of the children lurked behind the frames, trying to see what was happening. Adie jogged over to them, sweat on his brow, cheeks a hint darker, wheezing noisily. One of the girls, Liya, quickly poured him a glass of water as he began telling them what he saw. Everyone listened intently, except for Beckett who withdrew deeper back into their shared bedroom. Khari and Ember were biting their nails. Quinto embraced Emilia, shielding her eyes from the scene.

"Father," Ezme gasped as she descended from upstairs. She kneeled beside him, looping her hand over his thumb.

"I—"

"No, don't speak. Rest." She looked from Oliver to Victor who had dropped a jug on the floor. It crashed into chunks. She stared at Oliver in a desperate plea, stammering, "Bring a cloth and warm water...a string and a needle and bring...Help him! Don't just stand there like this, help him!"

The wound was too deep with Richard losing a lot of blood. Oliver knew there was nothing he could do. He met Ezme's glance with a slow shake of his head. She pressed her free hand onto Richard's stomach; Oliver's jumper had soaked through with blood and her hand now drowned in it too. With panic in her eyes, she started to shake her head as well.

"No," she mumbled, "this isn't happening. Oliver, do something! You know what to do!"

Richard groaned, "Ezme, it's time. There's nothing—"

"Don't say that. Don't you dare say that!" she snapped, her jaw becoming rigid. Oliver approached her, putting his hands on her shoulders, but she shrugged them away.

Richard leaned in, whispering into her ear, groggily, "Let me die on my own terms."

"No...You can't mean that. You'll be okay, it's just blood. A little bit more than...than we're used to." She gulped. "But nothing we can't fix. Right? We can always fix things. We have to..."

Richard's breath turned rugged, heavy and tired. Oliver adjusted the pillow behind his back to propel him up, making him comfortable.

"Not today. Today we don't fix anything. Today we welcome something new. Just give me—" he coughed, blood sputtering from his mouth in a wet drizzle against his palm.

Victor pushed a ceramic mug with fennel submerged in hot water into Ezme's hand. She unbuttoned her long-sleeve tunic, reaching for an ampule from the sewn pocket on the inside. She tipped it over the brim, mixing powdered poison into the steaming brew.

With shaky hands, she brought the mug close to Richard's mouth and he slurped a couple sips. The poison burned like a lit matchstick as it swashed down his throat. Angling his head to face Oliver, he whispered, "Take good care of her."

Oliver nodded once. "You have my word, sir."

Richard pulled out a locket, resting in the middle of his chest underneath his clothes, breaking the thin steel string free from his neck and searching the air for Ezme's warm hand, locking her fingers around the circular encasing.

She leaned in. Her hair spiralled around his face, devouring his last whispers. With a heaving breath, he glanced at her, and smiled, bowing his head down a little, letting his eyelids fall shut.

Ezme inhaled sharply as she straightened up, glancing around the room. Oliver took the mug from her hand and Victor ushered the peeking children back into their room. She could still hear the faintest sound of chatter amongst them through the wall as she scraped her father's blood off her skin, washing it off in a bucket in the kitchen.

"Go after her and make sure she doesn't do anything stupid," Victor instructed Oliver when Ezme swung the door open, crossing the field and disappearing beneath the canopy of trees.

Oliver knitted his brows together, running a hand through his hair. "Are you going to be okay? He deserves a proper burial."

"I'll dig a hole, then you'll help me carry him," was all Victor said, dragging a shovel behind him, leaving a trail. He began digging when he found a big enough spot further behind the first row of trees.

"Adie," Oliver called out to the boy, who followed him immediately out the door and onto the porch, "why did you leave?"

The boy looked down at his shoes, the muddied soles becoming the main source of attraction.

"Adie, you can talk to me."

"Wherever I go, bad things happen."

A calculated look sprung on Oliver's features when the trees cast a flicker of a shadow on Adie's face. He lacked words of consolation, wetting his lips, keeping the boy at arm's length.

"That's not true. Nothing that has ever happened to you is your fault and I won't have you think it was. Adie, we're in this together. You're family now and family sticks together. I don't want you running away or wandering off without any of us. You've seen how ungrateful the world can be and I don't want you to get hurt. Do you understand?"

Adie's gloomy eyes shuffled to his feet again before Oliver pulled him into an embrace. He then asked the boy to help Victor, along with Beckett who was the first to dirty his hands in soil. Ember and Liya sat nearby, shaken up. The youngest child, Emilia, buried her face in her hands and wept, soft wailing dying on her lips in persistent waves. Khari, while trying to comfort Emilia, started hurling pearls down her cheeks as well, more dazed at the amount of blood she witnessed than anything else, suddenly feeling sickly and starting to look pale. Quinto had his mind set on collecting flowers, assembling them into a neat bouquet, tying a long grass knot at its stems.

Oliver didn't have to look long for Ezme. It took him mere minutes to get to the bottom of the stream, where water flowed pure, cascading into a rippling pool. She was sitting on one of the rocks, throwing flat stones in. When he approached and crouched in front of her, resting his arms on her lap, the light in her eyes dimmed as she looked blankly past him.

He searched, but couldn't think of anything to say, let alone find the right words. All he did was pull her hands to his lips, brushing them over her knuckles, then moved closer to her, wrapping his arms around her and letting his hand get lost within her curls, stroking them in a soothing motion. The way his mother used to do when he was sad. His arms offered her the warmth and safety she needed. She had let herself rest against the beat of his heart, trying to stifle a sob.

He whispered a gentle, "Shh…Let it out."

Tears trickled down her rouge cheeks, meeting their end at the fabric of his shirt. It was hard to relax her shallow breathing. She pressed her face deeper into his chest, sniffling.

"I need to go," she said.

Sour expression etched onto Oliver's face, comprehending the uttered words. "Go where?"

"Old Ruins."

"Are you out of your mind?" He pulled away from her, anger consuming his features.

"Possibly," she agreed. "But aren't we all?"

"No, we're not. I don't suppose I would do something as gravely stupid as this."

"I need more poison and your supplies are probably running low too. We need to stock up in case there are more deaths. It's the only peaceful way to go."

He stepped away from her, pulling his hands into the side pockets of his trousers, turning his back on her. "I didn't think I'd ever have to say it, but a lie is never pretty on your lips."

She hadn't moved. "It's not a lie. It's true." After a sigh, she admitted, "*Partly* true."

"Ez, I know when you're not telling me something. What did your father say to you?"

Within the locket, she found a rusty, old key chipped in half. The other half was missing. Oliver took it in his hands, examining it.

"He told me to *start at the beginning*."

"And you think Old Ruins is the place to go looking for answers? This is the worst thing to do in the current situation."

"And what exactly is that situation? My father dying at Isla's hand? Another Drishti? Many innocent lives being lost every single day? We have to protect them. Shield them. Do whatever we can to hide them."

Oliver's hand closed around the key, hard. The jagged edges dug into his palm.

Ezme's breathing softened when she said, "What I need right now is to go and see her. While I'm there I might as well bring home more poison. Oli, I have to do it."

CHAPTER 6

Convulsed in deep sleep Cassandra's limbs jerked. Fingers stroked the silk linen beneath her, slipping the blanket onto the stone floor. Groggily gawking sideways, she realised it was the middle of the night and the whole castle was fast asleep.

Slowly lifting herself up, she rested on her forearms watching the huge clock on the wall *tick, tick, tick*. She slipped her legs over the bed's edge and tiptoed quietly towards the dresser with a blanket around her bony shoulders.

She stepped into the corridor outside of her chamber to the sound of bottomless snores coming from a guard, asleep on a stool. His head tipped over, one hand plummeting down towards the ground with the other over his stomach. She edged around him, steps quickening down the spiral staircase.

When she reached the bottom, she turned right. She gasped when a pair of cold hands touched her skin, prickling the ends of every nerve like icy blocks. Cassandra managed to swivel around, catching the cashmere blanket from slipping down. All the same, her heart pounded as she engulfed a deep breath, a shudder passing through her body.

"Claudette," she managed, covering her nightgown securely. "I'm on my way to the kitchen for a warm brew. I couldn't sleep," she lied.

"I will prepare," the maid said and shuffled towards the kitchen taking the corridor to the left.

Cassandra's eyes longed over the dim lights at the end of the corridor she intended to take and reluctantly followed the maid instead. Claudette placed a duster down on the side of the table, lit up high candles on the rustic candelabra, and reached for an iron pot hung on a metal hook above a huge timber kitchen island.

When the maid finished brewing the cup of chamomile tea with lavender strips, she took out a jar of mild honey, and excused herself to dust other surfaces. Cassandra plucked a honeycomb out and dropped it in her tea, watching as it dissolved.

She waited long enough until she could no longer hear feet shuffling or furniture being moved before she grabbed the cup in her hand and set off towards her original destination. She had a feeling the portraits on the walls were watching her, eyes following her movements, knowing what she was about to do and judging her for it, but she couldn't simply go back to bed.

As she sneaked into the dungeons, she was hit with the smell of damp earth and decaying stone. The cell was secured with a key only Queen Isla and her personal guard had access to. Within the thick metal bars, every man had a hardened wood bed for himself with no cushioning and only a few scraps of material to keep warm.

The contents of a little ampule from her pocket spilled into the lukewarm beverage and Cassandra lifted her eyes to look at Cree, the sickly Drishti prisoner.

"Please, drink this," she said, extending the cup in between iron bars separating them. "Please," she repeated. "I don't want you to die. This will help. It's medicine."

Cree didn't lift his eyes to meet hers. Instead, he eyed the cup and grabbed it with shaky hands, spilling some of the liquid clumsily over the brim and onto his feet. He coughed, trying to cover his mouth with the back of his hand, then lifted the cup up to his lips.

"Don't drink it," Hunter interjected. Cassandra and Cree's eyes diverted to him. "You'll die."

"W-what? W-why would—"

"She wanted to help you, fool," he snapped, narrowing closer to the bar, catching her eye. "But this is not the way to do it. I'd rather not see you dead right next to me."

"I only wanted to," she paused, scrunching her eyebrows together in defence, "ease the pain."

Spills of the brew wet her hands as Cree shoved the cup back into her grip, excusing himself away from her and laying down on the cold ground, facing the bleak, chipped wall. His body was shaking from the fever.

She turned to Hunter. "There's nothing else. Look at him! He will die within the week!"

"He barely drinks. He will die of dehydration before the fever takes him. He needs warmer clothes, more water to drink. Only then he can recover. Bring him a wineskin. Fill it with elderflower and white willow bark brew."

"We don't have white willows within—"

Hunter narrowed his eyes at her, almost mocking her, "There is one just outside the castle grounds."

The prisoners were sometimes allowed to take rounds around the northern edge of Blackwick town, at all times watched by the guards with their weapons drawn at the ready. Cassandra couldn't venture outside the palace, she was hardly permitted to even visit the markets within the castle unless she sneaked out, hidden beneath a cloak. Even that didn't happen very often.

She had been caught too many times before to risk it again. Hunter liked watching the willow grow older with him; branches spreading out and falling to the ground, giving him a sense of time.

He continued, "I'm sure a princess can whip up a speciality brew on a fake cough. If you want to help him, I suggest you do it fast."

"You don't understand," she said, shaking her head. "She knows everything. She always finds out."

Cassandra glanced around the cell; others were asleep or pretending to be, laying silently on their beds. She yanked her head meaningfully sideways for Hunter to approach the bars closer.

She lowered her voice so that only he could hear her. "You know I can't do that."

"Then it's just a matter of time."

Her cheeks prickled a hint darker. She was about to open her mouth again to explain why she couldn't, why even if she tried to help someone, her mother would do something a lot worse, but Hunter already turned his back on her. He propelled himself against the chaffed walls, his eyes sticking to the floors until she finally disappeared down the corridor and back into her chamber.

She stared into the dresser mirror, silently arguing with her subconscious, before resigning back under the warm linen of her bed, trying to forget about Cree.

It wasn't until the morning that Cassandra drew the curtains open and looked through the window – straight into the meadow within the castle walls, stretching between a garden and the stables. She saw Queen Isla with two guards on either side of her facing a line of Drishti suitors, one of the men on the ground on all fours.

She threw on a coat, tightening the knots all the way up to her neck, leaving her chamber and stumbling down the left corridor, turning a few corners to push open a huge door to a balcony bathing in pleasant sun rays. The tables were lined with a white cream cloth and the cutlery had been set out, but apart from a jug with orange juice, there was nothing out yet.

She edged around, her hand sliding down the balustrade, tracing the stairs down. Her hand smoothed out her hair, hiding the messy ends under the collar of the coat. She took a quick, but steady breath to compose herself before approaching her mother.

"I wasn't expecting you up so early," Queen Isla addressed her.

Cassandra scanned what was happening. Cree was on the ground in between Isla and the line of Drishti suitors. He was huffing, his hands smeared with dust. Before him was a patch of blood he coughed up. She passively looked over him, bowing her head slightly down to the folds in her coat and the wrong choice of shoes she had picked up in a hurry. She tried to hide them under the scuffs so her mother would not notice.

"It's almost time for breakfast," Cassandra replied. "I saw you out my window and wished to join. What is happening here?"

"This man here doesn't belong in line with the others. He is sick and we simply cannot have a sick man in our ranks." Isla folded her hands one over the other in front of her. "But I gave him a chance. A hundred laps from the stables to the garden and he may stay. He doesn't seem to have what it takes to be one of your suitors."

Cassandra's glance fell briefly to Hunter, who shuffled from one foot to the other. "How many laps has he managed so far, Mother?" she asked nonchalantly, brushing away the immediate response to crouch down and help Cree to his feet.

"Middle of lap fifteen," the guard to the right replied after receiving an approving nod from the Queen.

"What if he doesn't finish it?"

"I think you know the answer to that yourself, dear. After all, you're soon to decide the fate of the rest of them that are not chosen," Isla said sweetly, gracefully reaching up to touch Cassandra's chin.

Cassandra was about to curtsey and excuse herself from the terrible procession before witnessing something she didn't want to. Out of the corner of her eye, she saw dust swivel from under someone's boots and her head turned to him. Queen Isla slowly followed suit, measuring the man from top to bottom.

"Your Majesty," said Hunter, bowing his head, then meeting her eyes. "Let me finish the laps for him. Spare him."

Cassandra swore in her mind, her neck and shoulders tensing in anticipation as she flexed her fingers by her sides. All Queen Isla did was walk around Cree to face Hunter. Cassandra withheld her breath. There was a certain seriousness about him that unnerved her. Combined with the void of his pensive, black eyes and the apparent lack of fear of consequences, he appeared calm and collected.

"I'll run the laps for him," Hunter said again, looking directly at Queen Isla this time. His eyes unwavering. "Let Princess Cassandra decide what happens with her suitors when they're not chosen. After all, isn't that her first decision as the Queen-to-be?"

Isla squinted against the sun rays, smiling with a hint of mystery that was hard to decipher. "That won't be necessary," she said, clicking her finger at the guards to lift Cree up. "Take him back to the dungeons. Clothe him in something warmer and feed him."

The guard lifted Cree up, propelling him against his own shoulder, and led him away from the group. His legs weak beneath him and the sound of a wet cough prevailing from afar.

"Thank you, your Majesty," Hunter replied, bowing his head and stepping back into the line.

Cassandra took the hems of her dress in her hands and began to walk back towards the balcony. The varied scents of food diffused around her, but tasted bleak on her tongue. She wasn't hungry. Claudette took a knife into her hand to cut the warm loaf of bread, laying the slices neatly one on top of the other. She then passed a plate of turkey chunks, cut up radishes and plucked lettuce leaves under Cassandra's nose. Reluctantly, Cassandra's hand reached for a glass vase of chives to sprinkle on top of her sandwich when she saw her mother climb up the stairs.

"I'll be with you shortly," Isla said, rushing through the door and into the palace.

Taking a bite of the sandwich, Cassandra didn't realise Hunter had appeared on the balcony, his coal black hair was swept to the side and a smirk welcomed his face.

"May I say something?" he asked, his eyes quickly travelling from the plate of sausages to the plate with fried eggs, sweet cinnamon rolls at the far end next to a variety of fresh juices from the nearby orchards.

She chewed the bite, covering her mouth with a napkin. She gave him a sharp nod, raising her eyebrow.

"You look…" he began, trying to find the right words. "I just wanted to say that you look…"

She gulped down the bite, cleaning the corners of her lips with a gentle tap. She tipped her head to the side, interpreting his loss of words as a sign of flattery. "Yes?"

He cleared his voice, a half-smile playing on his lips. "Just that you look like maybe you should try using a brush. In other words, you look like shit, Princess."

He grabbed a vine of grapes from the table and plopped three into his mouth at once. He swaddled into the palace with his back pushing the door open, giving Cassandra a small wave with his free hand and a wink.

Claudette rushed across with a tray of tea, setting it down by Cassandra's plate and ripping through mint leaves to throw them in. She stirred the hot drink with a silver spoon, raising it out of the water and wiping it on a cloth sticking out of her waist apron. She dipped the spoon into a bowl of sugar, ready to stir some in, but Cassandra extended her palm out.

"It's fine. I don't want any tea," she said, trailing her chair from under the table and leaving the half-eaten sandwich on the plate.

In the reflection of the white framed windows, her hair was tousled with sleep, frizzy, and the ends stuck out in many directions. She lifted her hand to smooth it out again, but it just rose straight up anyway.

She hadn't had a good night's sleep by the look of the bags formed under her eyes. With her pale complexion, they looked a lot deeper than they really were. She had left her chamber so quickly; she hadn't paid attention to how she looked or what she wore. Her first instinct was to be involved in whatever was happening outside. She was still wearing her nightgown with a high lace neckline under the now unbuttoned coat and the mismatched shoes, but this didn't bother her. Hunter's comment did.

She noticed the rosy lip balm she was wearing was smudged over the outline of her lips. She wiped it with the back of her hand, wishing she had something clever to say back to him.

CHAPTER 7

"Be careful, alright?"

"You don't need to worry about me, Victor" said Ezme, throwing a leather bag over her shoulder, casting a glance at the children playing quietly outside, a game with rocks she never understood or learned to play.

As Victor sat on a tree stump to sharpen his axe, she turned to Oliver, perched atop the porch railing with a perfectly round pink apple in his hand, throwing it up and down.

"You're being stupid," he chided, taking a bite, sweet juice dribbling down his chin.

"I'll be back by tomorrow's nightfall. Can I trust you to not do anything stupid yourself?"

"I cannot answer that truthfully." He jumped down from the railing, closing the distance between them in the blink of an eye. "I don't know what will happen tomorrow let alone in the next five minutes."

She recognised the way a tender grin ran over the corners of his mouth, twisting upward in an unruly smirk, his eyes flying to her parted lips for a split second. Instantly, she shook her head, pressed her lips together and placed her hand against his shirt. She could feel how his chest rose and fell with a heavy sigh.

He stepped away, taking another bite of the apple. He then threw it far above and over the cabin. He added, "Like Victor said, be careful, okay?"

She watched him walk away and a part of her wanted him to turn around. To give her one of his charming smiles she could not resist, but he didn't. He kept walking until he was inside the house with the door slowly shutting behind him.

The bag sunk heavy on her shoulder despite its hollowness as she made it through Esteracre woods to the nearest opening of trees. Once there, she managed to spot a lone merchant with ceramic pots and bunches of flowers tied up the sides of his carriage. He had a dirty apron on, once white, greased with colourful smears from the petals, and he chewed a piece of wheat straw in his mouth.

"Good sir, excuse me!" She waved him to stop. "How much to take me to Old Ruins?"

"Old Ruins? Who would want to go there? My cart won't be going that far north no matter how many coins you've got to offer."

"Twenty coins?" she asked, holding a hand over her eyes to cover from the bleak sun rays. She spotted tiny sweat beads falling from his forehead into his eyes. He wiped them off with the inside of his elbow.

"I said—"

"Thirty? I have no more, sir. Please."

"Hmph." He spat out the straw, grasping the reins over his sizeable belly. "Zeffari's Keep. No further. I have business to take care of and family to get back to in time for supper." Just before he looked over his shoulder to a place she could occupy, he insisted, grumbling, "Payment now. I've had enough skiving crooks trying to hitch a ride for free."

Her fingers wound nervously around the strap of her bag, hoping her expression didn't reveal she had readily lied to the merchant. Another hundred and some coins sat in a side pocket, but only thirty were spare in another satchel for her travels. She would have to figure out a way to get back once all her money was disposed of and her bag filled up with enough ampules of poison.

As long as she had enough money, she refused to use her powers for personal gain, and even then, she would much rather walk the whole distance than compel an innocent person into doing something they otherwise wouldn't. Especially not for free. Nobody did anything for free within the land of Valeis.

She hopped onto the carriage and sat in between buckets full of forget-me-nots, pastel tulips and even a few singular roses with thorns cut carefully out from their stems. All it took was one whiff of the light, pleasant scents and her shoulders relaxed, leaning against the shaking wall.

The merchant murmured under his breath, bargaining with himself, "Blackwick market can wait for tomorrow.

The coins will tide me over until then. I might even bargain a few on the outskirts."

It was difficult to find roses in the wild. They would often peek in the windows of richer families; wilted petals falling, in a circular whirl, elegantly to the clean floors when it was their time to die, only to be replaced by a new batch the next morning. Death was lurking behind every corner and sometimes even stood in full view, poking its scrawny finger at an hourglass. Sand burying seconds, minutes, hours, days.

As the sun squared up right above the carriage, Ezme looked over the hills and yellowing grasses the further north they travelled. She left the merchant at the top of Zeffari's Keep, a rural town. The scent of warm bread caught in her nose led her feet to the source. An older woman in scruffs of rags tied roughly at her hips with a thick, black belt sat on the dusty road. Her skirt was patched up in different coloured fabrics. A few loaves were set out on sheets of parchment next to her.

With a warm mouthful, Ezme closed her eyes, remembering the stale slice she nibbled on last night. "This is the best thing I have eaten in weeks."

The woman didn't speak, just ushered her away to make space for anyone else who wanted to purchase the remnants of her baked goods.

It took Ezme the best part of the afternoon on foot. The last gentle brush of sunlight stretched across the ruins. Weather-worn stone pillars surrounded weeds and towering spires of cobwebs. The flutter of wings was the only sound, apart for the leaves rattling underfoot and an occasional rat scurrying across.

She found a hazel timbered cottage with a thatched roof in the heart of the Old Ruins, overlooking the Valeis castle on the other side of the lake. Faint drafts of smoke protruded from the chimney. Fresh footsteps were embossed on the gravel and a distinct rocky path led to the front door.

Ezme swallowed a sweltering eagerness to get this over and done with, but she held her hand up to the door rather hesitantly. The plan was simple; in and out. She was going to walk in, pay for the poison and walk back out, visiting Zeffari's Keep shelter on her way back home.

If only it were that simple.

A voice reached out from the house, melodic but firm, "Whoever you are, I do not welcome visitors. Turn your bloody boots the other way and keep walking."

"I'm here for poison," she murmured back, loudly enough for the voice to reach Aylie.

The door swung open and Ezme wasn't sure what awaited her within the cottage. It was filled with an overwhelming stench of hide scattered one over the other on the floor. An overhanging lamp from the ceiling that reached low to the ground suddenly burst with flames.

Ezme loosened her scarf as the woman pulled her inside, shutting the door and wandering up to a boiling cauldron. Rosemary, dill, pellets of daisies.

"Cup of tea?" she asked.

Ezme's brow shot up, with flimsy fingers she unbuttoned her coat and slid it down next to a row of herbs in lopsided handmade clay pots. There was no hanger. Everything was on the floor. Or on the walls.

"I wouldn't drink anything you'd give me."

"I suppose that's fair," she responded, and her low humming voice reverberated suspiciously in Ezme's ears.

Something stirred under the bed and soon the creature loomed through the distance to Ezme's feet, its eyes following hers. Hissing, scraping its claws on one of the skins, ready to pounce on her like a predator on prey.

"I guess not only the potion I created reveals a Drishti," Aylie spat the word out like it was a haughty, lethal curse, blackening her tongue.

Ezme kept a steady voice, recoiling her foot from the dreadful resemblance of a cat gnawing at her boots. "What did you get for it? Coin?"

"Fortunes don't interest me."

"Precisely," Ezme muttered under her breath, finally managing to throw the creature off her leg.

It jumped over the lamp, almost burning its tail, ran underneath Aylie's feet and landed on a scrap piece of cardboard, scratching its paws some more. Eyes sharp, never straying away from the direction of the door, anticipating something that wasn't there.

In the reflection of the burning cauldron, Aylie's features were soft with the exception of deep wrinkles forming around her tired eyes. Her hair was parched brown, as if left to dry out in the sun for too long, and put to one side of her shoulder in a muddled plat.

There was no easy way to say it but Ezme had to let Aylie know. "Father died this morning."

"About time. He shouldn't have survived for as long as he had." Aylie continued to stir the contents of the cauldron, slowly, as if she heard good news, then sunk a thin metal mug beneath the surface, filling it up to the brim. "Neither should you."

Ezme's fists clenched and her eyes narrowed. "You sorrowful woman."

"I'd watch your mouth if I were you." Aylie blew onto the liquid, then took a small sip. "Your kind is not supposed to stay alive…at least not for too long."

"You once loved him. Drishti or not, it wouldn't have hurt you to offer words of kindness, remorse, even the slightest emotion of any sort." Ezme picked up her coat, stuffing her arms through the patched-up sleeves. "Drishti are more human than you'll ever be."

"Words don't hurt me, my child."

"You lost the right to call me your child the moment you gave us both up to Queen Isla."

"And yet to this day, I still have no clue how you managed to escape from the hands of death, but as the old proverb says, '*Stupid always has luck on their side*.'"

Ezme forced her breath into a calming measure and thought of a little girl holding her father's hand, running through the woods, hearing murmuring voices and a shout, *"This way!"* Richard picked her up and continued to move in the opposite direction until his legs could walk no more. It was the two of them. Two of them straying away from death for as long as they could manage. With Ezme's grey eyes, he couldn't seek shelter; anyone could turn on them and call Valeis guards to seek them out and dispose of them. Ezme would never forget the exact way a nasty leer painted Aylie's face as she stood in the doorframe with her arms crossed.

"What do you want?" Aylie finally asked, sticking the tip of her index finger into the cauldron, then with a hiss cooling it down in her mouth.

Ezme cast her a glance. She was wearing a layered floral dress with colours that didn't quite go together. The bottom layer was navy, the middle was bright pink with hints of green stem embroidery. On top, she had a black laced, well-worn leather vest. It was cut out in spiralling loops and circles by unskilful hands with a blunt knife, bound together by two thin fabric belts knotted at the waist and near the collarbone.

"Have your stores run dry or is the healer boy needing more resources to kill people instead of saving them?"

Ezme stomped through the mess and laid the satchel next to the cat on the tabletop. "Hundred coins."

"I'll give you one dose for a hundred coins."

"What?" Ezme managed, raising her eyebrows in defiance. But as Aylie ignored her, proceeding to tend to the potted herbs, she added, "What is it you want in return really?"

"A series of tasks," she hummed.

Ezme considered. Whatever Aylie wanted wasn't going to be easy. "One task."

"Four."

"Two."

She plucked a root from a pot and replanted it into a bigger one. "Maybe three?"

"Two," Ezme repeated, her patience at its end.

"First one is quite easy," she hummed again in between her words. "I need a few square stones for these pots. Five. No – six! Yes, six will do. I can lay them around like this," she said, trailing her nail in the dirt around the plant. "Search outside."

Ezme ran a hand over her forehead, sweeping her hair upward. It was ridiculous. "And the second task?"

"The second task is also quite easy…"

Aylie sauntered towards a fur-lined coat on a straw filled bed, reaching into its deep pocket and pulling out a vial; coils of colours mixing in and out.

CHAPTER 8

Oliver waited an hour before he set off behind Ezme, but he didn't follow in her steps. Instead, he carried on east, past Easteracre woods with the sun setting above his head. The silent trail was interrupted by a noisy yet diligent woodpecker until he reached a clutter of houses a stone throw away from each other.

The town saw a handful of elderly people swaddle with metal buckets of fresh stream water. Others had fishing rods by their sides, empty buckets ready to be filled up with trout and, if they were lucky, not-so-common shiners.

"Morning," Oliver greeted a pack of anglers by nodding in their direction as they babbled on about different kinds of earthworms and other nightcrawlers for bait.

As he slid in between two houses that almost shared a wall, he saw a friend standing in the doorframe, waiting with his arms at his hips.

"I knew you'd come today," he said and hugged Oliver, patting him on the back heavy-handedly.

"You can't possibly have known…" Oliver began, then smirked, shaking his head. "The roof. Of course."

The thatched roof needed patching. Oliver glanced up to see a tool bag perched upon the roof's ridge, along with the top half of a bottle of unidentified brown liquid.

"I'm not usually superstitious, but the old witch said she'd rather me fall from the roof trying to patch it up than drown in the stream fishing again."

"You fell in again?"

"It was a big one. I almost caught it, but then *splash* and there I was. Knee deep in the waters, fighting with that slimy damned thing." He slammed his hand on his thigh. "It got away," he said, shrugging his shoulders in defeat. "So, I decided to stay home today. Time to fix that leaky ceiling before the old witch chucks me out the house."

A woman yelled from inside, "You call me an old witch one more time and I'll curse all the shiners in those waters never to swim near you again."

Oliver chuckled as his friend lifted a finger to his lips, ignoring the comment. Moments later, Oliver was riding further north on his friend's carriage pulled by two horses. Tugging the reins close to his body made the horses whinny and set off at a faster pace. He slowed down when the crisp air whistled with notes of pine, and his breath became visible, spiralling from his lips. The steep and exposed bedrock proved slippery for the hooves, so he turned the horse the long way around through patches of granite rocks surrounded by erosion.

A hill stretched out before he glimpsed the crooked hut's roof. It looked as if it was trying to hide from him, crouched low in the bare ground. As the horses reached the peak of the hill, he jumped down from the carriage and led them closer to the hut.

Don't do anything stupid.

Coarse, uneven stones made up the walls of the hut and one side seemed taller than the other. The roof was made out of corrugated iron, overhanging from the walls. Thin puddles crackled underfoot, the bitter cold seeped through his clothes making his bones numb and he cursed himself for not bringing an extra layer underneath his flimsy coat.

Hidden underneath one of the stones was a key. He unlocked the door, giving the handle a forceful push. The hinges creaked. Peering into the darkness of the hut, he moved cautiously inside, the sunset protruding from the window. He gasped, his hand moving to his chest, as a dark figure walked past it.

"Damn you, Blade!"

She responded, her voice coming from behind him as she closed the door, "That might teach you not to break into my home again. Guilty conscience equals guilty reaction." She threw herself onto the sofa lined with different sized coats and thick shawls in many different colours, entwined in a rainbow mess.

Oliver slipped out of his coat, rubbing his hands together in an attempt to warm them up. "As if I'm going to take moral wisdom from you."

"I have my mere human instincts trained. Nothing startles me." She watched as Oliver's gaze fell upon an unlit hearth. "Since you're here, you might as well light it. I'm not particularly fond of the terrible draught."

"What gave you the impression that living in the mountains might be warmer than in the South?"

"Don't get snarky with me. After you've warmed the place up, I might spare a few moments to listen to why you're here before I simply kill you."

"For such a small frame, you're awfully feisty," he noted, throwing chunks of wood into an empty chamber. His laughter echoed between them, thawing her rigid posture as she threw her legs over the sofa's arm.

Ashes fluttered upward, but before the wafts of smoke escaped, he locked the iron enclosing, letting the fire stutter slowly to life. He gazed at the glowing embers, rising up and down within their confinement, wondering if locking Blade and Ezme in the same room would solve their bickering.

If only it would result in the same understanding he and Blade shared when it came to business, or whenever one of them needed something, he may have given it a second thought. Whatever caused their grievance, Oliver preferred to bite his tongue than dwell on it for too long, staying away at arm's length from invoking any truce between the two in case he made it worse.

After the flames engulfed the wooden chunks, the hearth protruded draughts of smoke from the chimney and warmth circled around them in the small, nonetheless, cosy hut.

"It sure is a long way to travel up here," she noticed, dragging her hair across the side of one shoulder and fidgeting to form a braid. Quickly giving up and shaking the tangles free to fall onto her back, she added, "What do you want?"

"We need to overthrow Isla's rule."

She stared at him as if he spoke another language. She opened her mouth to speak, to say something that made sense, but all she managed was a simple and strained "What?"

"We've lived long enough to realise that what Isla has been doing is wrong. It's no longer a battle between right and wrong because it's always been just one way – the deceitful and horrible way she stays in power by killing innocents," he continued. "And what exactly is the purpose of protecting children from death if all they know in life is to be frightened and to hide? In the end they will die anyway – sooner or later they'll find themselves in the wrong place at the wrong time. This is not life. It can't be."

"Oliver," she stopped him. "We are *not* Drishti."

"*We* are not, but you are aware half of the kingdom is made up of Drishti. At least that was the case before the killings began again. As long as Drishti exist – Isla won't rest. No matter how well they hide. Not only does she have access to a potion that reveals Drishti, but she's been crossing all sorts of boundaries in the way the land of Valeis is run. Richard died yesterday."

There was a pause and an uncomfortable feeling in the air. Blade stilled, listening to him. At the mention of Richard's death, her hand gripped around the shawl, tight.

"This is the time to use your skill to do something worthwhile."

"I live quite comfortably," she murmured, but as soon as she said it, she perked up on the edge of her seat, letting the thick burgundy shawl tumble down to the floor. She added, "But—"

"If it's a matter of money," he exhaled, "name it."

Blade realised it wasn't a matter of money anymore, or even survival. There was someone else that might be in trouble without the slightest idea. Blade's blood suddenly raced, grasping at Oliver's words, damning the knowledge Drishti could be recognised with a clever liquid.

The potion changed everything.

"Ride south with me. To Esteracre. I can offer you two hundred coins. Even three if that's what it takes for you to help us."

"These walls are too high, even for a fox," she said, a frown darkening her complexion.

He shook his head slowly. "One thing we both know is that you're not an ordinary fox."

"I can handle a blade and a few morons, but what makes you think I could kill a queen? Skill or no skill, what you're asking for leads to certain death. And nobody needs money when they're dead."

"What do you want then? Eternal glory? Songs about you? Or should I name my future offspring after you?"

"Don't be ridiculous. That won't be necessary."

His brow quirked up. "Why? Is it a bridge you want instead?"

He caught a glimpse of a smile lifting his hopes up, but as soon as they appeared, they came crashing down when she said, firmly, "No, Oliver. Not this time. I can't help you."

She got up and quickened her steps around the room, picking up a huge knitted grey scarf and a blanket. She chucked the blanket at Oliver while she wrapped the scarf around her body.

A puzzled expression turned his head sideways before she said, "You can sleep on the floor."

Silver mist settled on the mountain tops, the white paint barely visible on the sharp peaks, as Blade drew the curtains together. There were risks she would take but risking her life in such a careless way wasn't one of them. She lived long enough to know they don't stand a chance.

And mere three hundred coins wasn't the prize that would make it worthwhile.

CHAPTER 9

The castle gate loomed before Ezme. Coated in black with a speckle of gold ornate with thick, heavy chains on either side. It was pushed wide open, seemingly inviting.

Ezme gaped at it absently, rubbing her hands on the sides of her trousers. The frayed hems on her chunky knit jumper began to bother her and she pinched them, trying to hide the scuffs back into the sleeves of the coat that felt too warm, although her breath was visible in the air.

Inside her pocket was a vial with a murky potion she dared not open. A step away from revealing her magic. She clenched her fists until her fingers turned white, clicking her knuckles. Her boots sloshed through a puddle as she set her eyes on one of the guards patrolling the entrance. She prayed, hiding her hands inside the depths of her pockets, not to be exposed as Drishti. She could hear Oliver's voice in the back of her head telling her to turn her boots the other way and leave.

Her feet marched onward, swaying hesitantly at first, but when the guard caught the sight of her hooded figure, her muscles tensed up and she fought against crushing the vial in her hand. Her feet desperately wanted to flee, to run.

She had never been to the castle gate before and although she was expected to feel fear, instead she felt a tickle of excitement pulsating in her veins, racing her heart. Something she hadn't felt since sneaking out of Esteracre cabin before the age of thirteen. This was uncharted territory, yet a certain pull tugged from within to come closer.

Nothing to be afraid of. This is a simple exchange.

Potion, that could potentially expose me and get me killed, for some coins. Simple. Nothing to be afraid of.

She repeated inside her head for the words to etch themselves in her mind, over and over again, until the guard huffed, touching the hilt of his sword at the hip.

The tip of Ezme's nose lifted as she held his gaze for a moment longer than she felt was necessary. Swallowing the uneasiness, she added quickly, "Aylie has sent me to—"

But before she could finish, the guard shuffled his feet together with a *clunk* at the metal bound heels and left his post. Another man replaced him, immediately holding out an expectant hand. She fidgeted with the potion, then dropped it in his palm. Seizing it, he held it up to the sun before stashing it inside his breast pocket. Then, a small brown package, wrapped tightly around with a white twine replaced the emptiness in her hand.

Until now, she hadn't looked at the man properly. His trousers were black and there was nothing at his belt; no weapon, no means of attack or defence. He seemed harmless. His shirt was dishevelled, the bottom sticking out from under a waistcoat that was a few sizes too big for him.

She spun on her heel to leave, but his iron grip latched onto her elbow, turning her back around to face him. Her eyes fixed on his prominent collarbone, a burning discomfort inching up her throat. She kept a neutral expression, shifting her gaze back to the ground; back to the muddy boots she needed to scrape clean when back home.

"Look at me," he requested.

He extended two fingers planting them on the bottom of her chin and lifting her head up to look at him. His cheeks were sunken and his olive skin dry and dull. Tired circles were etched beneath the black hollows which were his eyes. He was young. Black hair, a pointed jaw and white pearly teeth.

When he spoke, his voice was low, almost melancholic, filled with a sense of pain, but his eyes told a different story. Uneasiness settled on her shoulders like a heavy weight.

"Tell Aylie we'll need more. By noon in a couple of days. Now go. Hurry along, and you'd better make your paces quick," he warned her.

Ezme nodded, her heart collapsing in her chest. He let go of her chin and waved her away with a bored flick of his wrist. She imagined he was still looking at her, burning a hole in her back. Cold air brushed her cheeks in a raw pink sweep and her thoughts spiralled. The need to get away as far and as fast as she could turned desperately into a jog as soon as she disappeared from the view of the gate.

She couldn't shake off the immerse sparkle of recognition the moment their eyes met. Immediately, she knew he was Drishti, and with that it meant he knew she was one of his own too.

She weaved through bustling Blackwick town to the surrounding fields, sticking to the lower parts of small hills, crossing a handful of standalone cottages on her way back to Old Ruins. Looking over her shoulder every few metres, the sun began to sink, and the tower peaks of the castle were out of reach; she had to squint to see them buried in the clouds above, the darkness devouring the fields whole. Edginess set in her chest, clamouring slowly up to her throat in short gasps of panic.

She wasn't far from Aylie's cottage. Her steps became heavier and slower, angling around the outstretch of barren woods laden with huge tree trunks felled by lumberjacks. She stepped over smaller branches, feeling them scrape against the trousers covering her calves, and then she heard a growl.

A slow. Vicious. Dangerous growl.

She swallowed, picking up a bigger, heavier stick, lacing her fingers around it with a firm grip, turning towards the resonating sound. There was nothing there. She slowly stepped backward, careful not to trample over the fallen trunks, keeping her body rigid, bending her knees a fraction.

"Go away!" she shouted into the midst of an empty, thick mist creeping amongst swaying branches, praying against the sudden chill that any noise would scare the mysterious animal away. Whatever it was.

She lowered her weapon after minutes of staring at the dried-up bunches of swaying weeds, then jolted towards the near edge of the lake where a stony path led to Old Ruins. Before her feet made contact with the surrounding gravel, a dark shape jumped in between her and the disappearing reflection of the lake. Glinting sharp fangs blinded her and her knees trembled.

"Go away!" she screamed again, her voice faltering a tone too high.

The wolf gathered his paws together, keeping his jaw below the shoulders as close to the ground as possible. Ezme caught sight of his bared teeth. The threatening nature of pointy bloodlust edges sent a chill down her spine. The growl vibrated through the ground reaching up to her limbs that shook as a result. She waved the wooden plank in the air, then threw it at the wolf. He pounced to the side, scuttling his tail in between his back paws, nearing his steps towards her once more.

It was at this moment she looked into his icy blue, beady eyes, pleading in an afraid whisper, "Don't hurt me."

Like a charm, the wolf hid his teeth and rested his head on top of his paws, his tail digging into the gravel.

Ezme's throat became dry. She ordered, extending her palm in front, "Sit."

The wolf perked up, then sat down, staring at her with a tilted head.

"Roll over?" she asked anxiously, moving closer.

A smile played on her lips and she had an urge to let out a laugh the moment the wolf did what she asked for.

"It's not possible...It shouldn't work on animals," she whispered in disbelief, her hand now stroking the thick ashen mane behind one of the wolf's ears.

The wolf followed closely behind her along the path to Aylie's hut.

"Don't tell me you got yourself a pet wolf," said Aylie. "Just like your father," she moaned under her breath.

She slashed her fingernail through the brown paper to unravel what was inside the package Ezme brought back. A satchel of coins and an offshoot of a plant Ezme didn't recognise. Probably just another unique and completely unnecessary plant Aylie wanted to fill her cottage with.

Ezme drew closer, suddenly willing to stay longer. "Father had a wolf?"

Not knowing that about her father proved to her there were things he hid from her and she wondered what else he never mentioned. One time she had sneaked out of the house with Oliver, she remembered having a feeling something was following them. Oliver claimed he saw a tail once, waving a fire torch around to scare any predators away, then laughing at how paranoid she was. She had pushed those thoughts away, blaming it on her imagination.

But what if it were true? Had her father known all along that she sneaked out, having his wolf follow her? To keep an eye on her and protect her if needed?

"He had a wolf," Ezme muttered, staring into churning black smoke coming out of the cauldron. The burning stench made it hard to breathe. "Was there," she paused, not sure how to ask the question, "anything else?"

Aylie drew the curtains sharply aside, ignoring Ezme, unlatching the window and taking a handful of stones from the small bucket near the wall. She chucked them at the ashen wolf lurking closer and closer to her door from the ruin arcs bathing in the last scraps of the evening sun on the barren hill. She took another handful.

"Don't hurt him!" Ezme hissed, the vein on her wrist pulsating with anger.

"It will be okay. It's used to it." Aylie's fingers flicked the stones back into the bucket, one by one, unhurriedly. "What's its name?" she asked, climbing onto a tipping chair, collecting small vials from the highest shelf. "It has to have a name. Everything has a name."

Ezme frowned, observing Aylie closely. "Aylie. Listen to me. Was there anything else about Father?"

"Name. Give me a name."

"He doesn't have one!"

Aylie swayed from the chair onto the floor, sitting down cross-legged, spreading the vials over the layered skirt and beginning to carefully tip powdered poison into them.

She urged, "Well, just pick one. It has to have a name."

Ezme perched upon the sofa arm, hearing it crack under the pressure. She scanned the hut for inspiration. Her stare fell briefly over a stash of alluring dried up gypsophila, once pure white flowers, entwined with a long slick hardened blade of grass.

Now, their whiteness was a memory that turned into a blanket of ash. Their colour reminded Ezme of the wolf's mane; speckled with a furry, ashen coat.

Ashen.

His name was going to be Ashen.

CHAPTER 10

Cassandra rolled her eyes. The light sky she could see through the wall-lined glass windows was dotted with a few clouds, thick and fat, pacing slowly from frame to frame. Long queues edged forward to the entrance of the castle, nobody speaking about anything else other than the big day coming up within a fortnight. Even reluctant stall keepers turned their heads to see what gifts were being sent from other kingdoms, opening their ears to any gossip they could later retell in taverns.

"Coronation, my dear, is going to be the happiest day of your life," said Queen Isla, sitting upright on her throne.

It was lined with a golden pleated frame and shimmering charcoal cashmere fabric. The crown she wore had a Valeis pommel incorporated into the design with fire peaks burning around the circumference of the head.

Isla's tone was overly pleasant with a half-smile on her lips painted in an unlikely mirage, although Cassandra heard the hint of reprimand in her words. "A good queen pretends she's happy even if she'd rather be doing other things with her precious time."

The longer the procession took the more Cassandra gnawed on her cuticles, bouncing her leg up and down under the overly colourful dress Queen Isla made her wear. Every now and then, she stared at the ugly red lipstick slapped on her mother's lips returning her attention to new shoes filling the marble hall to be replaced by another pair, and another pair.

Beyond the tall door she could hear excited chatter silenced every time the guards let another person in. By the time the procession was finished, the hall was full of gifts from all over every town and even other kingdoms, including a pastel orange fabric that caught Cassandra's eye the moment she saw how beautiful it was, catching the faint daylight within its folds.

A tray of cakes marked a quick break. After taking a bite from a lemon-infused sponge, Queen Isla turned to Cassandra, placing her hands squarely on her lap.

"I have chosen your suitor."

The door swung open and Cassandra's shoulders shifted to face her future husband. She could see his huge eyes from afar. She nodded at him in acknowledgement, feeling her mother's watchful eyes observing her reaction.

After a polite nod, her eyes trailed from the peak of his hair all the way down to his polished shoes. He did not look scruffy like he had a few nights before. Instead, his collar was pointed up and sleeves stowed away within the waistcoat's pockets, decorated with a golden thread.

"Admirable choice, Mother," said Cassandra, returning her attention to Queen Isla.

"Hunter will be escorting you between your duties today and he should not leave your side until the day of your coronation."

A faint smile distorted Cassandra's peaceful composure in a painted lie. The syllables monotone, spoken many times over the years: "Very well, Mother."

The morning turned into a relentless afternoon – she had to stand perfectly still while a seamstress kept pushing pins into the pre-cut pieces of fabric, trying to keep the design together with her thin fingers zooming in and out between the elaborate cuts and folds.

In the corner of the room stood Hunter.

Perfectly still, perfectly silent.

Cassandra scowled and his eyes flew to her immediately. A worried crease appeared on his forehead, then ceased as his eyes darted from the Princess onto the dull, white wall. The seamstress pushed a pin into Cassandra's knee, withdrawing her hand quickly when she heard a hiss and felt her hand burn. The Princess swatted the clumsy hand away, stepping off a raised pedestal and watching herself carefully in the mirror. She could feel how Hunter's stare bore into her back and made her skin crawl.

Cassandra's breath flew from between her lips as the black-rimmed brown corset was pulled tightly, too tightly, squashing her ribs. Their stare met in the reflection of the mirror for a moment, but his brows were drawn together in an uncontained composure. It was a mixture of amusement with contempt, painted on his face with thick, hard brushes. The look was quite different to the one on the balcony where his features were relaxed into a boyish smirk.

Another woman fussed with laying down a simple, elegant tiara on a small cushion, waiting to place it on top of the Princess' head as soon as her hair was braided from each side. She reached for the blonde strands, separating them into parts.

"Don't," Cassandra snapped, "I want them to naturally fall down my back. None of that braid nonsense."

"But Queen Isla said—"

"I am going to be Queen within a fortnight."

The hairdresser sunk her head low, scanning the porcelain shoes Cassandra was wearing, picking up a comb and slowly brushing through her thin, silk hair.

Cassandra couldn't wait to be finally out of the wretched room where everyone fussed around her, about every single detail, watching her every move. She ushered everyone out of her closet and changed into a linen tunic, sewn with a pattern of colourful petals, cut out chiffon sleeves, and a pair of trousers tucked into knee high leather boots.

Hunter stood by the door, his back turned to her to allow for privacy, waiting to escort her into the kitchen for an afternoon tea where her mother would join. However, Cassandra flung the door open and marched into the opposite direction.

"We're going somewhere else," she instructed. "If you're going to marry me, we should at least get acquainted better, don't you think?"

He followed behind her reluctantly, answering curtly, "My sole purpose is to enable you to bear a worthy heir."

"If I knew you were so much for romanticism I would have asked for a better suitor. And there I was thinking that you would at least try to charm me."

"It's pretty hard to want to charm someone who had you locked up all of your life," he snorted. "Living in fear is not my definition of a happy life."

"And yet you don't strike me as someone who's afraid," contemplated Cassandra, laying her hand flat against the huge palace door, turning to look into his black, narrow eyes. "Besides, I am not my mother."

"You are to be Queen. You will rule the land of Valeis. Sooner or later you will end up just like her. Power-hungry. The problem is that you don't see it as a problem. It's just your way of life, always has been."

"I am *not* my mother," she repeated through gritted teeth, pushing the door open and stepping outside. She upturned the collar of her cloak to shield from the drizzle of rain that cooled her face. "I—"

"You tried to kill that poor man a few nights ago."

"It was for his own good!" she protested.

"Like I said," his tone was measured, deprived of emotions, "you don't see it as a problem."

"I didn't—"

"I don't need your explanations. We both know what my purpose is. I'd be lucky if I still have my head by the time your heir turns a week old."

"I don't intend on killing you."

"I don't intend on falling for any of your lies and I assume there will be plenty of those to come. After all, you have had the best teacher there possibly could be."

His words only seemed to have sharpened the edge of her temper. She walked under the arch, passing a line of guards that had their eyes on crowds that were much bigger than normal even after the procession had ended and everyone was expected to leave the grounds.

"Where do you think you're going now?"

Cassandra briefly turned to look at Hunter, raised an eyebrow, marching onward. Her coat billowed behind her like a winter's breath.

"We're supposed to stay within the grounds!" he shouted behind her. When she didn't stop, he was forced to follow her.

"Show me the way out," she demanded.

He brushed it off. "I don't know what you're talking about."

"I know there is a way out from here and not through the main gate, so take me there. Now."

Hunter's eyes followed the sky hawk circling in the sky above them, unmoved by her demands.

"Please," she added.

Under the crumbling wall was a small passage leading out of the castle onto the nearby lake. Cassandra jumped from one of the rocks, her legs slipping from under her. Hunter caught her at the last second, grasping her waist with one hand and then pulling her up by her elbow with the other. She heaved herself back onto two feet.

The blush on her cheekbones deepened in shame. "I don't need your—"

"You would have hurt yourself and I would have had to explain why I wasn't looking after you."

"Will you ever let me finish my sentences?" she grumbled, kicking a few loose stones aside, then supported herself with a hand in between a small slither.

"Where are you going?" he repeated, following closely.

"I don't really feel like spending time with you if you're going to be so prejudiced against me."

"I'm not prejudiced. It's just the way the world is."

"Prejudiced. I'm not the arrogant and power-hungry princess you take me for."

"I never said you were arrogant but come to think of it now I'm not so sure."

Cassandra stepped into a small rowboat at the edge of the lake. "Coming, or staying and watching me from a distance?"

"I'll let you know that I am only coming because—"

"Because you have no other choice? Heavens forbid I would drown, and the blame would fall on you?" she mocked him.

His lips settled into a line, but he lowered himself onto the boat's foremost plank, waiting patiently whilst

Cassandra fumbled with a rope anchored to the tree, refusing to help her.

"You do that a lot," she said.

"Do what?" he asked.

"Interrupt me. It's not fun being interrupted."

She pushed the boat off the coast with a wooden paddle, taking a seat and resting it on her lap. They floated across the lake with water rippling at the bow of the boat. She looked at him, long and hard, but he only tried to avoid her gaze, looking somewhere far across the surface of the lake.

"You're going to be my husband and yet you hate me."

She was met with silence.

"It'll be easier if you didn't hate me and we tried to get to know each other better."

"Listen," he grabbed the paddle from her and harshly broke the surface of the water by sinking it over one side of the boat, "whatever you're doing, I prefer we talk as little as possible. There is no point in that."

"No point in being civil with each other?"

"No point in trying something that will not work. Better hold off on any ideas you may be getting."

"We are to be married, Hunter. Married."

"It's nothing I've chosen for myself, is it?"

"Ouch," she whimpered. "I get that you'd rather be free, live your life away from here, wishing you'd never been caught in the first place. But I sometimes wish I were free too, you know?" She looked behind her shoulder at the castle. "From all of this madness."

The castle, while mysterious and stunning in the day, looked menacing after sundown. The peaks of the towers appeared threatening and Hunter's stare fell briefly upon the highest tower that hid secrets he was afraid to share…for now.

She continued, "You, me. We're not that different."

He gave a short mirthless laugh, then said, "You will end up killing people."

"And whatever have you been doing? Standing guard at the gate and pointing out all those Drishti born? You're as much of a killer as I am to be."

"It's not the same. I didn't choose to do that."

"You did. You choose to save your own life at the cost of others."

"Whatever you think you know about me, keep it to yourself. In the end, all men for themselves. That's how it always has been, hasn't it?"

He gave his head a small shake. There was a momentary flash of an unidentified void filling his pupils before they shook back into complacency. She met his gaze, holding it until something plunked beneath them in the waters and she jumped in her seat.

"Relax, it's only some fish beneath us," said Hunter half-heartedly, finding humour in the way her face scrunched up and her hand came up to guard her chest in defence.

She realised his anger wasn't directed at her but at what she represented, and she lowered her chin down, absently agreeing in her mind. She had to find common ground with him to dampen the uneasiness between them. He had been chosen as her suitor and there was nothing else either of them could do about it.

"Is it because of your brother?" the words left her mouth before she could bite her tongue.

She knew she had made a mistake when Hunter dug the paddles deeper into the murky waters and rounded the boat towards the shore. The sloshing quietened their thoughts.

"You don't know what you're talking about," he barked.

"Then tell me!"

The rowboat lodged within the ground and he jumped out of it, leaving Cassandra behind.

He ruffled through his slick hair, clasping it in his hand. He stopped and turned sideways to her. "You don't know about half the things that go on and you think you know me."

"There are things you don't know about me either. My path isn't laid out with rose petals," she said calmly.

His palms twisted into fists and he punched the air. Once. Twice. "Heck with petals! If I wasn't chosen as your suitor, I'd be dead within the next few days. What makes me so special to have been chosen over anyone else in that line? Was it because of all the sacrifices I made to protect my brother?"

Cassandra stepped over the edge of the rowboat, clutching the hem of her dress as she waddled over to him through the mud.

"I don't know," she sighed. "I don't know."

He scrubbed his face, sliding his palms down until they left his chin and he curled his fingers over his collar, pulling it slightly away from his neck, loosening it. The beam of the evening light, a narrow sliver over the horizon, illuminated the brass buttons on his waistcoat.

They stood apart from each other for a long moment, until the pain in his chest cracked away into tiredness, slowly finding the courage to look at her. Her face was an oasis of understanding although he didn't deserve it. She didn't know him, yet there was a ray of warmth within her normally cold blue eyes. He hadn't seen it before, but it was there. She didn't have to be watchful of her every step, every word around him and he felt his anger uncoil when her hand rested on his forearm.

"It's getting cold," she muttered softly.

"Let's get back," he lowered his head, giving it a half-shake.

It was a few hours later when Cassandra heard a hesitant knock on the door of her chamber.

"Come in," she said, slipping on a nightgown over her shoulders.

"It's me." Hunter popped his head in.

"I know. No one else would be permitted to even knock and my mother…Well, she would just walk in, wouldn't she?"

"I'm supposed to sleep here," he said, closing the door behind him and approaching her.

She clambered onto her bed, under the covers, smoothing the ridges out. "It's not sleeping that you are supposed to be doing here tonight," she said, her voice catching a slight wobble at the end of her sentence.

Hunter said nothing, taking his coat off, hanging it over the dresser chair, leaving his shoes by the wall. Cassandra observed the way he undid a couple of top buttons of his shirt, then turned away from him, curling up at the edge of the bed.

"I know I have certain obligations to fulfil in the role of your suitor…"

He paused for a moment, taking a long look at the smooth skin of her shoulder that protruded from under the cover, then continued to take his shirt off. She listened to his quiet movements around, until she felt the bed sink when he sat down.

"…but I won't force anything on you," he finished.

He pulled on the covers lightly and she released the length she had hoarded. He slipped under it, patting it down and resting his head over two pillows, face up.

The low murmur of his voice reached her, reassuringly, before they both fell asleep, "Not unless you want me to, Cass."

CHAPTER 11

The mare galloped onwards with Blade in its saddle. The wind wisped its taupe mane back when they reached the plain of the land between Esteracre woods and the burnt down ruins of the Lorkeep shelter.

Right before the Crossroads, the mare snorted and rapidly dug its hooves into the gravel, attempting to stop at once before a boar. It flicked its ears back and forth, stomping, and Blade felt its back muscles tense in fear. She laid one hand on its neck, gently caressing it to calm the horse down, her other hand firmly wrapped around the leather reins, keeping her knees pressed against the sides to prevent herself from falling off.

"All that fuss about a stupid boar," she exhaled. "It won't hurt you."

She then shifted her weight forward and burrowed a heel into its side. Like a charm, the mare inched around the boar, then picked up the pace, galloping through dry grass.

Reaching the castle walls, she glanced quickly towards the iron-wrought gate and led the horse east to rest beside a lake. She patted the mare's snout as it neighed, making sure the knot on the rope was tied up properly, giving enough slack for the horse to be able to reach the water.

She added, "I'll be back soon."

Right outside the castle walls was a town called Blackwick with its well-known market; open from dawn to dusk. Only the finest merchants could progress further into the castle square to provide for families with respectable standing; Queen's servants, guards, and the Queen herself.

One thing Blade liked about crowds was how easy it was to disappear in them, to become invisible to anyone who blinked. One step to the left and she was long gone from anyone's sight.

She dulled out the mixture of different voices but one.

"To pay scum like you more than three coins is robbery! ROBBERY! You hear me? That's all you get from me and I'll be on my way," a man bellowed, spittle flying everywhere. The buttons on his waistcoat threatened to burst open with yet another breath.

Ostentatiously throwing three coins to the merchant's feet, the man grabbed a bag of grain, then stuffed the pouch full of money back into one of the pockets and turned to leave, grunting displeasingly as he did so.

It was a quick reaction. Blade didn't need to think before her slim fingers zoomed out and slid into the man's pocket without him noticing. She held her index finger up to her lips and winked at the merchant, then placed three more coins on the wooden panel between them. Before he found the words to thank her, she was gone along with the crowd, dispersing between them like a wave washed up on shore.

A bridge of many stone arches led to the church on the uphill. It sat high, overlooking the city, like a watchful guardian with its wings sprawled in the form of peaks at either side of it, almost invisible in the misty parlour.

Blade sneaked through the front double door into an unsettling silence, tracing the Valeis pommel with the tips of her fingers on the brass handle as it fell into place behind her with a slow and menacing creak. The east side of the church was covered with cream white sheets, limiting the light pouring in. The west side was uncovered, brooding in darkness.

"Get out," she heard, and her eyes narrowed towards a girl. Loose rags covered her lithe posture, accentuated with a black corset. She let her hand rest upon her waist, piercing knives in her eyes. A type of edge difficult to handle, even by Blade, but her stern expression relaxed as she recognised the girl behind the voice.

"Where is he?"

"There is no one here that would like to see you."

Ava scowled as Blade pulled her head back, her ring catching on the short dirty blonde hair. "Would you like to try this introduction again?"

"Nathe! Get down here," Ava yelled, spitting the words out with vileness.

As the steps on the marble floor upstairs echoed, Blade released her grip, but Ava moved closer, inching a breath away from her ear.

She said through gritted teeth, "If you hurt him again, I swear to all that I know—"

"You'll slit my throat and all that rubbish we both know won't happen? Move. Away."

Ava succumbed to the wall, picking up a bucket with paint filled to its brim and proceeded to step onto a crate next to another mural, filling the pieces with jagged strokes of a paintbrush before her hand steadied into a smoother motion.

"Do you ever make any friends?" Nathe asked with a hammer in his hand, a long sleeve shirt was rolled up to his elbows. He brushed away the sweat from his brow, standing at the top of the stairs.

"All the time. Practically everywhere I go," she replied.

As she followed him upstairs, her eyes moved over his uncovered collar bone, a few buttons undone from the top. Ava muttered something under her breath, her hand stroking the murals angrily again.

He crossed his arms. "Why are you here?"

She bit her upper lip, eyes darting between his eyes and a hole in the panelled wall exposing brick beneath for a moment that seemed to stretch impatiently. She brushed away the little ball unwinding in her chest, forcing it to stay tied up.

His fair hair had scraps of ash grey and flecks of brick red and she wanted to walk up to him and pick them off. A scratch on his jawbone made it jut out more, his arms built up from manual labour. All she wanted was to slide her hand into his and feel the calluses beneath hers.

Perhaps it was her sharp tongue that made him notice her all those years back.

Before she pushed him away.

Before they became strangers.

There was something in his eyes she hadn't known. Something that looked at her differently, in a certain way she began to loathe the longer he stared at her.

"Why are you here?" he repeated, enunciating each word carefully.

She shook her head, looking at the dark west side of the church. Shadows seemed to creep in and pop out of the shattered windows. There was a slim line of red, but it wasn't paint, it was blood and that's when she realised his elbow had been sliced open, wetting the rolled-up sleeve in a rich colour. "I shouldn't have come."

Suddenly, she was aware he had a stronger weapon than she could ever hold when he spoke the next words.

"One thing I'll agree with." Sharp. Poignant. Bitter.

She bit back, "For someone who loved me, you've become terribly unbearable."

"I could never love someone who was fleeting at every opportunity." What he didn't say was '*someone whom I never had.*'

His words refused to bounce off her skin and instead, etched themselves somewhere in her chest. She deserved the way his words tore her apart, but this wasn't about them. He was the only person she cared about more than herself.

"I need to warn you," she managed.

"I don't need you to play my guardian angel."

He lifted the hammer and with one swooping motion, dug a nail into the wall, and another, and another, dulling out the silence between them.

"Nathe, you know I wouldn't have come here if it wasn't…"

Important.

She owed him that much. A simple warning – a heads up so he was aware of the dangers ahead. She owed him after she rode away from the warmth of their home, from the warmth of their bed, from the warmth of his heart.

"Meet me in three strikes at The Honey Brew," he said, and the metal clunked against the wooden panels again. "I might have some business for you."

When she descended the stairs, she could feel Ava's stare burning a hole in her back, but she didn't look at her. Step after step, she pushed the heavy door outward to welcome grey stones beneath her shoes, bleak pathways ahead, air filled with ash. It seemed to have come with a waft of something burning in a firepit from the other side of the church.

She looked back only once, searching for the topmost window but, to her disappointment, the view was obstructed. All she saw was withered vines clung to the outside walls, gnarling their way through the broken windows in desperation to be noticed.

Her feet quick and silent on the cobblestones led her through the streets and she didn't realise when she shouldered a handful of villagers on the way, their snarky mouths filled with words she didn't care for. Murmurs ricocheted off the walls in the quaint village as Blade stepped over a sewage spill running over her path, holding her breath from the litter dumped on the streets, sprawling with rotten vegetables and bad fruit.

She spotted a girl sitting on a rug, a few scrolls of parchment and a singular black feathered quill laid out before her knees. Her hair was covered in a dark shawl, the trimmings ripping across the hems, a few strands of black hair protruding onto her cheeks. The side of her face was darkened, purple.

Blade loomed over her for a brief moment before crouching down, attracting the girl's attention to lift her head up. "How long have you been sitting here?"

The girl stammered, "I need to sell the quill and scrolls before I can go back home."

Blade shifted, lifting the quill up. It was a regular quill. One she could buy for a single coin, two at most. And parchment? Parchment was even cheaper.

"How much are you selling them for?"

"I need ten coins," she responded. "Then I can go back home."

"Can you write?" she asked, searching the insides of her pockets as the girl nodded. "I want you to keep both the quill and the parchment. Keep writing, keep practising your letters. It's a treasure to be able to read and write."

She grabbed the girl's hand into her own and as she left, the girl's stare fell onto a pouch full of coins. The pouch Blade had stolen earlier at the market.

CHAPTER 12

White walls, dark wood with sticky residue of ale and men in furry coats lining up against the bar to get a drink was the last place Nathe wanted to be. Crooked candles and tattered lanterns suspended from the ceiling offered a dim, heavily nauseating mood.

Blade ambled into the belly of the tavern, securing a place in a corner booth stained with glass rings, hidden behind a wooden beam running diagonally from the middle of the ceiling to the far wall.

There were better places to meet someone, but Blade only wriggled her nose at the smell of stale beer and body odour, struggling with a broken handle on the iron-clad window, letting a bit of fresh air in to fill her lungs.

Her eyes flicked and, past a dirty cloud of smoke coming from a thick pipe, she saw Nathe's silhouette outside; tying a horse close to the water barrels, securing the double knots firmly. He stepped into the tavern, raised his hand to the maiden then, brushing the wafts of smoke away, took a seat across from Blade.

"Where did you get the horse?" she asked, observing a tender grin billowing to life and running over his lips.

He chided, "You think you're the only one who mastered the art of stealing?"

"Unlikely for you to steal a thing," she riposted, tapping her finger on the table, impatience seeping tangibly in the air between them.

"A lot has changed," he murmured as he shifted his gaze, focusing on the faces around the tavern.

"You seem nervous."

He turned his attention back to her. "Not at all. I just like to see who's around before I get comfortable."

"A trick you learned from me."

A moment of silent understanding passed between them before a tavern maiden approached them. She loaded two jugs onto their table, spilling the foam over the edges clumsily, a permanent smile painted on her lips in a rosy shade.

She wore a striped full-length pleated skirt reaching all the way down to her battered brown ankle boots. A cream shirt with puff sleeves was bound together by a satin ribbon across her waist all the way up to a lifted cleavage. Strings of messy hair spilled over her bare shoulders as she tossed the coins into the pocket of her apron, tied low around her hips. Nathe's eyes followed her all the way behind the bar.

Blade rested her hand against rough oak coasters, carefully running the tips of her fingers around them, aware of the poor attempt of filing away the likelihood of splinters. Dark draught cooled Nathe's palm before he set the jug back down, wiping the foam from his lips with the back of his hand.

"You still got it," he observed, pointing a finger at her wrist.

She turned the leather bracelet to face her, watching Nathe's blood whirling in the small bound capsule. She considered him before admitting, "It offers me protection."

"Glad to hear I've been useful to you on at least one occasion," he muttered, finishing the contents of the jug the second time he lifted it to his lips.

A ridge etched in between his eyes as he folded his arms expectantly.

"You're in trouble," said Blade.

"Aren't we all? Danger lurks in every corner these days. Avoiding it is simply a skill one can acquire like any other. Stealing a horse, for example, or even knowing your way around the woods away from deadly growls…" he listed, counting on his fingers.

"I heard Isla has a potion. A potion that can cause a lot of trouble."

He closed his counting palm, knocking it down to the table and running his other hand up his forearm all the way to his shoulder. "You really thought I didn't know that already?"

A tinkle of glass on glass sounded through faint music that grew louder as the crowd grew more comfortable, intoxicated by spirits and beguiling ladies on their arms. Someone danced, a woman, whirling her arms in the air as if possessed by a trance. The dress hugged her figure and heavily made up eyes held the stares of other men long after the music grew dull.

Blade reached for the jug, encasing it with both hands before taking a small, sour sip. "You said you had some business for me," she said.

"Quite possibly," he murmured absently, his eyes shifting from side to side.

He put his hand up for another draught. This time when Nathe's stare lingered on the maiden, Blade let out an annoyed breath, slamming her hands on the table when he turned her eyes back to her.

"Are you serious?"

He raised his hands up in defence. "Can't a man have a little look?"

"I feel like you're doing it on purpose." Her shoulders rolled back and she lifted her drink, taking a few more thirsty sips.

"So easy to ruffle your feathers," he chided with a boyish confidence that shot angry arrows through her bloodstream.

He stood up and took a seat next to her now, throwing his arm around her, burying his head into her hair.

"What are you..."

The words died as she felt his lips so close to the nape of her neck. A warm flutter of breath skimming across.

"Shh," he whispered while his other hand sneaked a piece of paper into Blade's pocket. "I heard rumours that there is a huge sum waiting for someone to steal a certain crown," he continued, playfully sliding his nose from the base of her collar all the way up to her ear.

His hand had slid inside her thigh and she picked up the game by relaxing her shoulders and slouching against him, but her hand grabbed his with a gripping force and brought it down to her knee where she left it be.

He continued, "Inside your pocket, you'll find a sketch of it. For someone like you, this shouldn't be a problem to sneak inside the castle, nick it and leave before anyone notices you."

"Getting into the castle is not a problem but getting anywhere further is certain death and I don't have a death wish, Nathe."

"There is a man that can help you sneak in. Name is Oren. You want to find him, but I'd prefer if you didn't mention my name. You might burn my bridges."

His hand trailed a little further up from the knee. She didn't jerk away this time. Instead, she drove her hips into his, letting him feel the rough hilt of her blade. In a warning.

"And you really don't want to burn my bridges." His words, unfiltered, entered her ear with a small shudder.

She crossed her legs, letting his hand slip away as she pulled away from him, inches away from his dark eyes. One of the eyes seemed lighter than the other while the seconds stretched between them.

"Oren," he muttered, shuffling his hips away, feeling a form of a small indentation from the blade. "Don't forget the name."

He downed his drink in one go, taking the jug with him to the maiden himself, smiling at her with a lopsided grin. He knew Blade was long gone.

And just as he expected, when he turned around, she wasn't there. Just a half-finished drink and empty, but still warm seats.

With a swift motion, Blade swung her leg over the saddle and all that was left behind her was a swirling dusty path as the mare galloped on. Not once did she turn to look behind. The residue of ale was still bitter on her tongue and the coldness of the liquid left a tickling, feeble cough for hours later.

She pulled the reins sharply to the side. Thick clouds wallowed over the canopy of a dense thicket she flashed through in the blink of an eye, reaching the final outstretch of a grim meadow leading up to her door. She shoved her shoulder against it to wedge it open, shutting it with a longing echo. The brittle walls trembled, and she grunted to clear her strangled throat.

After fetching a thick blanket over her shoulders, she let a small, iron kettle boil, gurgling quietly in the corner of the room, hung over blazing coals. She tried to clamour uneasy thoughts back into a box she willed shut and forgot. Thoughts about Nathe clung to her skin like a disease she had no antidote for; spreading in an unwanted spiral.

Blade sank her lips in a smooth beige mug, tapping the ceramic glaze with her nails, sipping on roasted coffee beans she managed to steal the other day from the market. The shopkeeper was focused on preparing the next cotton pouches for women and men who jingled their coins at him, his eyes gleaming with excitement at a promise of a prosperous day. What he omitted to pay attention to were Blade's quick fingers, lifting a coffee pouch tied at his belt.

She fell asleep.

CHAPTER 13

Ashen leaped through the woods, scouting his path ahead. Ezme picked a fragile stick from beneath her boots, playing with it in her hands until it crunched to dust, leaving only brown flecks on her skin. With Ashen by her side, she could protect the children better and make sure they were pre-warned of any upcoming danger.

With a smile on her face, she watched his tail trail ahead of her with both ears firmly up, listening for any nearby rustles.

Suddenly, Ashen stood still atop a rock, his paws sinking into the soft moss. His head jerked back, and he let out a howl; a long, distant sounding cry. Ezme's eyes blinked in disbelief when she saw a cloud of smoke above the canopy of trees.

Esteracre cabin was on fire.

Her home, a place where she had grown up, was burning.

A sharp, shooting pain in her chest knocked the air out of her lungs, realising she wasn't there to protect the children. She was late. Moments too late.

She ran as fast as she could with Ashen close by her feet. Clumsily, she tripped over a rock, tumbling down and scraping her knee on hard ground and crashing her palms into a stinging nettle patch. Ashen perked his ears up and impatiently poked her arm with his nose. She winced, pressing her hurt palms onto her sore knee.

"Go, Ashen," she said, "go and help them."

Ashen pounced over a fallen tree and sped off into the distance until his tail vanished from Ezme's sight and she staggered slowly onto her feet.

By the time Ezme reached the cabin, everything seemed to be moving too fast before her eyes. She immediately spotted a spike of hair belonging to Oliver enter the house, followed by heavy grunts and shouting. Whoever was screaming was in hysterics with a high-pitched voice shooting through everyone's ears. Ezme thought it might have been Emilia, but soon the shouting ceased and Ezme hoped that either Ember or Liya calmed her down.

Through the window, she could see Victor lift his axe and collide its sharp silver against a Valeis sword as their battle continued. His huge frame shielded the children behind him, keeping two guards trained on him by the narrow end of the corridor.

Ezme swore under her breath, looking frantically around for a way to help. The children were already supposed to be underground, in the safety of the bunker, and Ezme couldn't understand how anyone would have gone unnoticed by even one of the kids; their watchful eyes were always on the lookout, always hearing the tiniest of noises creeping around. The attack must have been sudden and abrupt. Whoever was in the cabin already knew about them.

The guards kept pushing, cornering Victor deeper and deeper. The children huddled behind him; fear splashed on their small faces. His free hand kept shoving them aside until they succumbed further down the corridor.

Ezme lost sight of Oliver. Then, one of the guards stumbled, barely holding his sword against Victor's heavy strike. The guard tried to propel himself up, grasping the sleeve of his companion who brushed him off and charged at Victor with all his strength, only to be stopped by sharp fangs sliding into his thigh.

Ezme ran to the door. Another guard charged at her from the side, reaching for the weapon at his belt. She swivelled around him, backing into the living room, behind the couch. Driven to the corner of the room, she held her bare hands up, ready to fight.

Huffs and shouts became bleak as she redirected her full attention to the guard whose sweat was dripping on the floor from the tip of his nose. The moment she made eye contact with him, the sword fell from his grip, a metallic echo sounding in her ears. His fingers curled and pupils dilated. Her hardened eyes flicked between hazelnut brown back to sharp grey before she blinked again, easing her thoughts into his mind, taking control.

Gently, as simple as breathing, she let the power seep through her, meeting every nerve until it reached the tips of her fingers in a relaxing sensation.

"Leave here. Right now," she ordered him before a blast, like a wildfire, shook her feet from underneath and she tumbled onto her knees, palms landing onto pieces of shattered glass on the floor, slashing her palms, small trickles of blood smudging the panels.

"YOU FOOL! NEVER LOOK INTO THEIR EYES," a broad-shouldered guard bellowed, his sword slid out of the man's stomach, who then spat blood, gurgling and falling down with a thud.

Ezme gasped. With his last moments, he tried to clutch onto the wardrobe, but his weight only pulled it over him, crashing him down.

She got to her feet in a matter of seconds. The guard weaved his bloodied sword in the empty space between them, keeping his gaze low, refusing to meet hers. As she blew a strand of hair from her forehead, a gust of smoke choked both of them and watered their eyes. The guard lowered his sword, wiping the itchiness with his sleeve.

There was a pulsating energy in Ezme's chest she wanted to let go of, but reality came crashing in, rooting her feet down to the floor. Learning the hard, unmerciful truths chipped at what she thought she was supposed to do all these years; hide and live her life in secret without drawing attention to herself.

But this could not be right. This was too far from living. It was admitting defeat and not standing up for oneself, let alone others. She couldn't let the Esteracre children go through the same path she had gone down. There was a much bigger battle to fight. Much bigger than what was happening within the four walls of the cabin.

The charred walls were beyond saving, ceiling panels dropping like flies. It was no longer her home. The corners of the ceiling smoldered and blackened with heavy wafts of smoke clouding around them as she stood over a man with a fire poker in her hand. She let it fall from her grasp. The heavy thud piercing her ears as the weapon fell on the ground was surprisingly soothing. It brought a wave of satisfaction for a split second before she realised what she had done.

Blood ran from the side of his head onto the floor and she closed her eyes, burying her own bloody hands in between her knees, crumbling towards the floor. Tears welled in her eyes and she cursed herself, deep down, for what she had done. For who she had become. She fought against justification that if it wasn't him, it would have been her. Laying there in the dirt. Dead.

The speckle of guilt engulfed her fingers in a fidget, and she rocked her body back and forth in denial. Then, someone grabbed her elbow and shoved her upward, forcing her to move. Her feet followed, but the shouts around muffled out. Blood ushered from her palms, scattering red drops in a trail behind her. She forced them against her chest to prevent her from leaving a mark and then her vision became black, finding herself underground.

She knew that part very well. Just like they practiced all these years. Over and over and over.

Inside the bunker, small hands wiped her cheeks and she saw the fabric turn red as long white candles, placed in brass speckled encasing, illuminated the darkened chamber.

She didn't have a scratch on her cheek, or at least she didn't feel it. An image flashed in her subconscious of how blood splattered onto her, marking the sin she had committed. The fire poker was still hot in her hands, burning as hot as coal.

She stared down at her own two hands. They shook, causing shivers to ripple down her spine. She pushed the fabric away and the small hands left her face in a hurry, dropping the soaked fabric onto the floor, leaving Ezme alone.

It was eerily quiet except for a sob that escaped Ezme's mouth, but she dragged a hand over her lips, shutting her eyes tightly. They could still hear a couple of footsteps above. They waited until the last set of steps dulled out before speaking to each other, the air turning moist and stagnant.

Oliver crouched under the connecting arch, laying his eyes briefly on Ezme. She was staring at the floor before her feet, slowly rocking back and forth with her hands entangled around her knees. The curls splayed around her face quietened her rugged breathing.

"It's going to be fine," muttered Oliver, patting Adie on the back. He tried to disguise it with a small smile although he knew it was a lie. Nothing was fine. Not right now.

Beckett was sitting in front of Khari and Liya, but he turned to face Adie. He encouraged, "Adie, come join us here. We can play a game in four."

Small hands grabbed the leg of Oliver's trousers and when he looked down, he saw a pair of huge, silver eyes staring back at him. As soon as he hitched Emilia onto his hip, she burrowed her head into his chest. She rubbed the tip of her nose with such persistence it turned sore pink.

A quiet murmur on her lips, "Oli, take care of Ezme."

Oliver rocked her up and down until her eyes felt heavy and her arms started to swing by her side. Victor waved them over, taking Emilia in his huge arms, softly caressing the side of her cheek and huddling her under his wing.

"It'll be fine, little one," he grumbled into her ear, plopping his own head against the cold wall and resting.

Although the deep cut on his shoulder was bandaged up by Oliver, it started to bleed through.

"Richard would be proud of us right now," said Victor. "We escaped death today."

"That we did," agreed Oliver.

Quinto and Ember each lugged a goat hide on either side of Victor and Emilia to keep them warm, while they joined the rest of the children, listening to Beckett change the rules to accommodate six of them playing instead of four.

"Recently, it seems to be lurking in every corner we turn," continued Oliver.

"An old friend." Victor gave his head a shake. "Richard once said death was better a friend than an enemy."

"He always said things like that. Quite the philosopher, wasn't he?" It was hard to notice Victor return Oliver's smile under his beard, but he did, reminiscing about his old friend.

"Remember the thing about lemons?" asked Oliver.

"To seize the day by its legs and squeeze it like a lemon?"

"Yeah."

They both chuckled until Emilia squirmed, drawing away from Victor only to make herself more comfortable by laying her head down on his lap. His hand covered her shoulder and he drew the hide over, making sure her feet were tucked in too.

It was time for Oliver to walk up to Ezme who hadn't said a word, her face still in her hands. He sat next to her, drawing near and putting an arm over her slim frame. He felt her shiver against his body, so he strengthened his embrace. He pressed his cheek to the side of her temple, just sitting silently with her, listening to the irregular beat of her heart.

With a hoarse, cracking voice, she asked, "Where is Ashen?"

"The wolf?"

She nodded slowly.

"Safe on the ground," Oliver replied. "Hopefully finishing what needed to be done."

A drip of water slipped through the cracks and nooks. It began to rain, and the presence of water meant that the cabin must have burned all the way down. Despite the unnerving trickling noise, the bunker's chamber seemed to have eased Oliver's and Victor's worries about the safety of the children.

They were all cradled by earth and relatively warm with enough provisions to last for days if needed. It was quiet, except for silent whispers amongst Beckett and Ember who were deciding on the warmest hide to sleep under.

Their whispers diffused and were replaced by Ezme's calming breath. Oliver hadn't moved, signalling Adie to bring the thick cotton blanket from within one of the crates by the far wall to fit himself and Ezme under. He then brought it over their shoulders and shuffled backward to lean against the wall, opposite from the ladder leading out into the world, bringing Ezme to lay her head against his chest. He rested his chin on top.

"Ez…" he breathed into her hair, kissing the top of her head. "Try to sleep. I'll be right here."

CHAPTER 14

A candle burned out by the time Blade rolled out from underneath an abundance of blankets that had kept her pleasantly warm during the whistling night.

A sharp dagger was the first thing from the table she tucked back into the sheath at her hip, securing a second smaller blade inside of her boot by the ankle. Before she made her way to the castle, she glanced back at the messy sofa she was leaving behind.

It was always Nathe who made the bed. She picked up the blankets one by one and rolled them up, stuffing them half-way into the gap of the sofa arm. She bit her lip, shifting her gaze to her horse as she walked out, pushing Nathe to the back of her mind.

"We don't need anyone, do we?" she mouthed while patting the mare's snout. From the confines of her pockets she produced a few sugar cubes the horse licked off her open palm. Hoisting herself up, she began her journey west.

Where a rugged half-fallen tree lay, Blade anchored the heel of her boot against its bark to lever herself up with the help of higher branches. She manoeuvred closer to the castle walls as she soared a jump onto crumbling ledges made of stone.

She hardly used this entrance, knowing Hunter knew about it too. The castle grounds would be a thriving place for thieves if they knew how to gain access within its walls. Finer food, finer clothing. Anything Blade could think of was there, a stretch away.

One thing Blade wasn't was foolish. She watched the guards change shifts, observed their patterns, learned that if she as much as approached too close to the gate, she would risk pockets full of jewellery to be exposed and forcefully taken back. Possibly with consequences she'd rather not test. So, she stayed away, only stealing from markets outside the castle walls.

Every time she caught a glimpse of a guard, their absent-minded yet alert eyes caused tiny trinkets of shivers up her arms as her fingers twitched and longed to feel a cool blade in between them, where it belonged.

She was standing in the middle of the grounds that buzzed with noise from the conversations among men, ladies in silk dresses, and merchants. The merchants weren't shouting what they were selling, trying to gain customers. Their customers had more money than they could imagine, their prices set high enough to only have to operate for a few hours each day to meet the day's earnings and go back into either the lower part of the grounds or to surrounding towns where they lived.

Blade didn't know what Oren, the man she was supposed to find, looked like. She walked through the middle of lined-up carts, her fingers itching at the sight of luxury items she could nip, but she held them inside her pockets, keeping her head lowered and her ears sharpened for mentions of names. To her disappointment nobody said his name.

Some carts were filled with silks and linens in beautiful varied colours with cherry blossom red being the most popular of shawls, followed by ocean cool turquoise. The spice cart didn't tickle her nose this time due to the quality of products and a cart of pies and cakes drew her in closer with a rare cinnamon scent and baked apple slices. The man spoke in a honey-glazed tone, bringing a lot of customers, the slices of cakes selling out very quickly. Blade spotted a pair of mice nibbling on the crumbs that fell onto the ground.

"Mother wanted a huge cherry pie, not some crusts with powdered sugar on top," a girl said.

"But Mother doesn't know these are better! She has to try them first."

The twin sister replied with a grimace on her face, "She won't be happy you spent all the coins on this dry piece of wood."

"Look at them." She held up a crisp pastry made of dough shaped like tiny angel wings. "They're divine!"

"They're cheap and not worth the coin you just spent!"

Blade chimed in, "I've tried them before. They are really good. You should give them a try."

"And who are you to tell me what to do?" The girl spun on her heel, crossing her arms and jutting her chin out.

"Ceila, leave it alone. Let's just go home now."

Ceila's nose couldn't be any higher. "Mother will not be happy about dry brushwood, but I'll let her deal with you accordingly. As for whoever you are, stay out of other people's business," she snapped at Blade and stormed off, her cloak billowing after her in angry whispers.

"I'm sorry for my sister. She has an ill temper. Would you like one?"

"Oh, that is so kind, but it's absolutely fine. Take them home. I hope your mother will like them. Sprinkled sugar makes all the difference, especially with a hot brew in hand," Blade said, attempting a wink, and the girl started to turn. "Wait a second! Can I ask you something?"

The girl waited expectantly, stuffing angel winged pastries in between a thin brown rag.

"Do you know a man by the name of Oren?"

"He's the wine seller. Other side of the market," she answered quickly, then set off on a run to catch up with her sister, turning a corner.

Oren spoke in a husky drawl that made Blade want to draw near him, just to hear every single word the man had to say. He was dressed better than all other merchants with a clean cotton shirt underneath a fur-lined coat with tasselled sleeves. A hat was covering the fact he didn't have a full head of hair anymore, but a bald patch running from the top of his head to the back with the thin sides still visible.

Irregular carafes were clear with a vibrant green liquid. Perfectly shaped decanters, however, were only sourced from the depths of aged oak barrels situated within the wheelbarrows, with its deepest red hues pouring out into the containers when a customer requested a piece.

"Nathe sent me to find you," Blade said. "He said you could—"

"Not here," his voice sounded harsher and the bubble of his calm and kind voice burst with a *pop* of sudden reality. Oren's jaw clenched, and his mouth fixed into a thin, petulant line. "Tell Nathe I send him my regards and that I don't appreciate him sending strangers my way for any favours he thought I owed him."

"He was adamant you could help. It's about—"

Oren's smile extended to a couple more customers piling behind Blade and he sidestepped her to greet them; his drawl voice returning and a smile springing up on his countenance in a welcoming warmth.

She climbed over the wooden bark that was his stool filled with different tints of wine and sat on top of an empty barrel that was tossed to the side. When Oren turned around, he gritted his teeth at her, reaching for an empty decanter to fill up with his finest wine.

After his customers dispersed, he hissed at her, "Go away, won't you?"

"You know what, Oren?" She cocked her head and drew one foot over her knee while the other flailed down, inches from the stone-paved ground. "You and I could actually get along if you didn't have so many layers."

"I have no interest in helping you."

"But why would Nathe send me your way if you didn't have anything valuable to give?"

"Go and ask that wretched kid yourself."

Blade's lips twisted into a scowl as she held her shin with both hands. She was inclined to ask more questions because the Nathe she knew was always kind and thoughtful and caring, but never wretched. Never. There was not a single wretched or evil string in his soul.

"I need to get into the palace and you're the person that can help me," she said slowly, staring into the merchant's hostile eyes.

A mirthless laugh began but was soon lifted from Oren's lips the moment Blade swooped down from the barrel and with the heel of her boot, slammed it down on his foot. He doubled over, unable to stop her from dragging a blade through a full oak barrel, seeing how the thick grape spewed and sloshed down to Oren's feet.

"Don't," he whimpered, holding his hand up, his eyes scanning the surroundings in alarm.

"The guard on the east side left a minute ago and the one on the west side has his back turned on us," she said, shoving the man up to face her. She inched a breath away from him. "My name is Blade. I'm sure you've heard of me?" she asked, raising her brow, waiting for confirmation.

He nodded sharply, wincing.

"You can either help or I'm sure I can spare a few moments to ruin your stash before you have a chance to shout for help, but by the time that happens, I will be long gone, my friend."

He whimpered, "I'll…I'll help. Please don't ruin my wares."

Satisfied with his answer, she pushed him. He stumbled against the wooden bark with his back, almost knocking off a carafe that wobbled dangerously.

CHAPTER 15

Blade was in. Past another set of high gates, past the second set of guards, within the palace grounds, walking carefully across the steep edges of the towers, holding onto a fickle rope hammered into the walls.

Silently, she descended to the lower edge and jumped onto the flat marble beneath. Her figure hid within the darkness offered by an arch casting faltering shades.

Not far from her, she heard two monotonous voices coming from what she thought were the stables with a huge barn door stretching high above the other side of the arch. Squinting, she could hardly make out their silhouettes; one standing, one sitting on what she presumed was a stack of hay.

Soundless and delicate steps led her to a half open door of the palace. Her fingers slid into the crevice and pulled them wider; just enough to fit her body through. The torches burned hot at the end of the corridor and her heart immediately spun whilst shadowed surroundings churned around her.

The trailing pools of bleak light revealed a line of guards on either side of the walls and Blade felt an unyielding flush, crouching down and retracting a steel edge from inside her boot, although there was no sudden movement. She sucked in a breath, holding it, waiting for something to happen. Daring for someone to step out of line. Only when she took a few cautionary steps towards the first guard in line did she realise it was just a hollow, rusty armour. Dusty and full of cobwebs and spiders living inside of it.

She bit down on her tongue, focusing on making herself invisible, silent, palms pressed softly around the edge of a wall as she sneaked onto another corridor. The stone walls were damp and cold against her fingertips.

Blade had known darkness before, but this didn't feel the same. It robbed her of the confidence she knew, deflating from the depths of her chest, as she knitted her brows together, focusing her breath. As she moved, her grip tightened around the smaller blade. She felt the other dagger brush against her hip in unison with her steps. It was a security blanket she could always rely on.

Family portraits were hung in gold plated frames, painted in colourful oils. In the dim light their shapes seemed to writhe, losing their tinge.

She strolled through the kitchen like a ghost. Quiet and invisible. A whiff of a roast chicken with garden vegetables entered her nostrils and her stomach grumbled. She gulped down the hunger, suffocating its scream, and carried on up the spiral staircase. She heard something and traced her steps back. Nothing more than a murmur. The maid's shoes clattered upon the floor.

Blade inhaled…

The maid brushed inches from her nose in a, once black, greying creased uniform, murmuring as she walked past, as Blade's posture melted into the wall behind a slab of concrete, keeping her eyes alert for any other movement in her peripheral vision and she found herself fighting hard against the instinct that whispered into her ear to do whatever it took to find Queen Isla tonight, even if it meant hurting innocents, but she quickly brushed the wretched thought away, scolding herself for, almost voluntarily, losing the moral compass she tried to uphold.

…then exhaled.

The clatter drowned out and Blade made her way up the spiral staircase, catching a whiff of a musky blend of fir and pine. And something else entirely – a refreshing citrus zest with a mellow spice undertone.

There was nobody in the chambers. What drew her attention to a mahogany drawer was an old map, stained with ink, a cross next to each village. Lorkeep had persistent red lines through its name like it never existed; erased whimsically.

Blade searched every nook and cranny of the bedroom. Her eyes fell on a tiara made of glistening, polished diamonds upon a velvet pillow in one of the top drawers. Her fingers brushed against it. She scuttled down by the drawer when the door etched open, then shut after a figure paused in the doorway. She heard slow, heavy footsteps drown out. She quickly took the crown and left the chamber. Hiding behind an empty suit of armour, the palace seemed entirely abandoned, except for two guards down the hallway.

"I wish I could take Ina to the ball next week," one of them said, his dreamy eyes staring ahead.

"Don't be stupid. When have you ever been invited to a ball?"

"It's the Princess' coronation. Maybe this time we'd be able to—" he stopped speaking as soon as the other guard laughed.

"Aren't you Prince Charming, eh? Better get this outta your head because it's not going to happen. Put your polished shoes back in the basement."

"I just thought…"

"Nothing is going to change. Queen Isla or future Queen Cassandra. It's all the same. Stay in line and do your duty. That's how all us common folk get by. And thank the heavens you weren't born a damned Drishti," as he said it, he spat with disgust. "Which reminds me," he shuffled, "go and check on them."

"Why me?"

One fierce look was all it took for the guard to get up and with heavy feet march down the hall, turning a corner into the basement. Wanting to follow the guard, Blade took the opportunity to create a distraction by knocking a metal wrist off the empty armour. As she did so, a sudden gust of wind entered the hallways and the guard hadn't moved, swearing at the blasted, never-ending wind he was beginning to grow sick of.

Blade reluctantly retracted her steps out of the palace, setting her curiosity aside. She had the crown, now all she needed to do was escape.

A handful of guards stood before the door, barring her way out, and amongst them, she saw the traitor who had ratted her out; Oren. He stumbled away into the night the second one of the guards tossed a pouch full of jingling coins up in the air.

The guards advanced on her in half a circle, holding their arms out as if attempting to tame a wild animal. She could dart sideways, climb the roof of the stables, find a way to jump down over the palace walls and safely slip back through the grounds towards the cracked passage she had entered through. She could do it before any of them had a chance to blink and realise she was running away.

But there was no time anymore when she felt heavy hands seize her arms from behind.

She was led back into the palace.

PART II

CHAPTER 16

Blade sat alone in the empty cell with nothing but a pool of water in the corner and a shattered glass she'd thrown against the wall earlier. All day she heard shimmers and a damp pleading uttering in her head with wishes to be let free.

She imagined hearing a church bell ringing somewhere close, reverberating in her mind.

Chime.

Chime.

Chime.

Keeping a wild animal in captivity weakened it and slowly chipped away its soul. Time passed slowly and she ran out of ideas of how to escape. It felt like being trapped within an hourglass except, instead of grains of sand falling and burying her – blood was dripping. Thick. Blade's head popped up when she heard the door rattle, swinging with a scratching sound against the cracked floor.

Someone muttered gruffly, "Is she Drishti?"

"Look at me," Hunter demanded, staring deep into her startled eyes.

She pulled down on her left sleeve with her fingers to hide her bracelet, but Hunter noticed it, letting it slip from the guard's knowledge, turning to him.

"She's just a common thief. Nothing more."

"We should cut her hands off so she doesn't do it again," the guard said, chuffed with the prominent idea.

"I'm afraid it's not for you to decide," Hunter snapped quickly, barring the guard's way to the cell's entrance.

Their stare met – Hunter glowered above the guard's head. The guard finally stepped away, extending his palms flat out in defence.

"You're one hell of a lucky bastard. Why they chose you to be her suitor, I'll never know."

"We're not friendly. You want to be careful with what you say around me," Hunter warned him, his fingers entangling the cell's iron bar in a hot flush of temper.

The guard bowed his head curtly and left the cell. As soon as the door closed with another heavy creak, a smile crept over Hunter's young features.

"Hello, old friend," he said. "Fancy meeting you here." He extended his hand to Blade. She ignored it. Her eyes only flicked from his face to his hand and back up. She took a step away from the iron bars.

"Give me your hand."

She squeezed her hand into a fist, letting blood ooze and drip from her cut palm. They could almost hear the gentle *tap, tap, tap.*

"Fine, suit yourself," he said, extracting two blades from the side of his trousers that he'd taken from the guard before they entered the dungeons. They clinked together. Blade's eyes glistened and she narrowed closer to the bar, her cheeks pressing against the cool iron.

"Give them back," she hissed, baring her teeth at him.

"There is no need for hostility. You'll have them back and I'll let you out."

She squinted, a question in her dry mouth sounding hesitant, "Why? Why would you help me?"

"I'm merely serving my own needs and, so far, both of us lived up to their ends of the bargain before. But here you are…within the castle walls. I seem to recall telling you not to come here ever again. Not one strand of hair fell from Nathe's head. In fact, he's doing a great job at the church, isn't he?"

Blade sensed a certain edge to his question that sent an uncomfortable shiver up her spine. If this wasn't blackmailing, she didn't know what was. A couple of years before, Hunter had been the one to drive her away from Nathe. She had refused to help him strengthen his relationship with the Queen any longer by informing on Drishti locations in Valeis, ultimately sacrificing her own relationship with Nathe. Hunter took away the only sparkle of happiness she had left by telling her that in order to protect Nathe, to keep him safe from Isla, Hunter wasn't going to point a finger at him being a Drishti, as long as she left him and never stepped foot in the castle.

"Running into you screams trouble," she replied.

"Then you seem to love trouble."

"Cut to the chase." She threw her palms against the bars, sending a metallic rattle around them. "What do you want?"

Hunter didn't flinch. Instead, he stood tall in admiration of her reckless confidence, watching as a trickle of blood smudged down the bars, slowly causing her pain the longer she gripped them.

"I need you to find someone for me and bring them here."

"Why can't you do it yourself? You never seemed to have trouble finding anyone if you really put your *mind* to it."

"Certainly, one of my many attributes," he grinned at her, "but I need her to come here willingly and I don't exactly strike people as amiable."

"One thing you're right about," she quipped and pulled her hands from the bars quickly when she saw Hunter try to catch her wrist.

"We could have been a good team. You and me. With your reflexes and your undeniable wit," he mocked.

"If only I wasn't restrained," she muttered.

"We're not enemies here," he continued. "I believe you may already know the person I'm looking for. I need you to bring her to me."

"Who?"

"If I'm not mistaken, her name is Ezme."

Ezme. A girl who seemed to be wanted by everyone.

"I know her," Blade blurted, suddenly interested in what he had to say. "But I don't want her blood on my hands. I've done enough of that for you before."

"No, no," he said, shaking his head. "I need her alive."

"What's so special about her?"

"I'm sure you know a lot about Drishti and our abilities. But Ezme's powers are even more unique. What she can do is extremely rare and I only heard about it once before. I thought it was a legend. Something you tell your children as a bedtime story. That sort of thing, you know," he began. "But I've never experienced quite the same feeling with anyone else as I did with Ezme when she happened to stumble across the castle gates just the other day.

"Well, I'm telling you this so you will understand it's not a whimsical request. This is important and having you here, behind those lovely, and I'd say pretty strong, bars, gives me a bargaining chip I'm willing to offer."

"I asked, what's so special about her?"

"You have no patience, do you?"

She leaned against the far wall, crossing her arms. "None at all."

"Ezme's blood comes from a very old, ancient family. I thought the family line ended years back, hence becoming a legend. But even I might have been mistaken. When I made a connection with her, I felt it. I felt the underlying energy I've never felt before within anyone else.

"She can not only control humans. She can control animals too. And certain animals can be a deadly weapon against even the most powerful of Drishti."

Blade kept her jaw rigid, taking the newly learned information with a stoic expression. She wanted to ask what Hunter wanted with Ezme, what his intentions were as to the powers she held, but she simply waited. Whatever game he was playing, she had to stomp on words as if she were balancing on a thin sheet of ice.

Less was always better.

"I believe you can understand why I'll need her. For change to happen, you need to do something."

"I think I understand it all clearer now. You don't want to die," she said carefully, raising her eyebrow, trying to search his eyes for an answer she was looking for, but there was nothing in his eyes that would give it away. "The Princess is turning eighteen soon and they have played the little game of who her suitor should be, but that's not the fun part, is it? The fun part is that you've become the unlucky man. Am I right?" she teased, a corner of her mouth twisting up. "I'm assuming, after the rumours of what happened to Queen Isla's suitor and the one after him, you don't want to die."

Hunter smiled, giving her the answer she needed. "Isla compelled huge numbers of common folk beyond our comprehension. She thinks she's unstoppable, securing the long reign over the land of Valeis. On Cassandra's eighteenth birthday she is to transfer everyone under her control to Cassandra and we need to interrupt that transfer. We need to break it. We need to kill the Queen."

"What if I say no?"

"I guess you'll stay locked up in here forever, or until the Queen decides what's to be done with you. But between you and me, I wouldn't count on surviving long with her decision. And as to what happens with Nathe, it always seems to come back to him in the end—"

"You mention Nathe again and I will—" she paused, pressing her lips together, fire speckling her eyes.

"I won't mention him again. He will be absolutely safe and so will you," Hunter promised. "That is, after the deed is done. Are you in?"

"How do we do it?" she asked.

"The castle will be filled with villagers and foreigners from neighbouring kingdoms during the coronation. It's best to strike then. No one would expect an ambush before the ceremony. But before I say more, give me your hand."

Blood was still ushering out of Blade's palm, starting to pinch colour from her cheeks. Although she didn't want to, she stretched her hand out between the bars for Hunter to wrap it up in a large handkerchief he produced from his pocket.

Hunter continued, "Getting into the castle for you alone is not a problem as you've proven so today, but you'll need my help getting others in. A pack of wolves might not be as easy to disguise either, considering you'll help Ezme gather them."

Blade swallowed. She wasn't fond of wolves. Even for her, they proved too strong and too quick. She avoided the parts of the woods and mountains she knew she could stumble upon them.

She said, "I assume you'll be at the gate to let us through."

"Only until noon, then I'm needed elsewhere. You must arrive before."

He looked up to meet Blade's calm blue eyes, waiting for an answer. She didn't say anything back.

"The coronation is in a fortnight from now. Actually, it's gone past midnight, hasn't it? That makes it thirteen days."

He let go of her hand and she inspected it closely, creasing her brow at the uneven bow he made to tie it up.

"If I give you your weapons back, will you promise not to kill me?"

"I'll try, but I should roughen you up a little before escaping, otherwise it will look like you just let me leave."

"Right," he muttered, "I knew you'd be ecstatic with this opportunity, but you could at least try to lessen that sudden flicker of excitement in your eyes."

"Well, what would be the fun in that?" she taunted.

He turned the key in the lock, at which point Blade pushed it against him, slamming him almost to the floor, but catching his hand at the last second to dampen the fall. The bar hit his temple, splitting his left brow vertically. She took her daggers, stashing one away in the folds of her jacket and holding one firmly in her left hand.

She pulled Hunter's shirt from under his trousers, ripping the hem with the slick of her blade and, as a good measure, she elbowed him in the ribs. The strike landed hard enough that it sounded as if something cracked and he grunted, curling his hand to cup the area where it hurt.

"Ever so graceful," he spat, wincing. "Straight ahead, then turn the corner and take the third corridor on the left. You'll be out by the rear of the armoury. It's not guarded, but there might be someone lurking around so watch out. Don't get caught again. Make sure no one follows you."

"I thought I could just walk out the front gate?" she mocked.

"Just shut up and go already." He flailed his hand at her. "Go."

Blade followed the corridor out and just before exiting the palace, she heard a clatter on the marble flooring. She peered her head around the bend. Queen Isla was walking towards the dungeons and Blade's hand flew to her chest pockets, tapping them fervently in frustration because the crown was with Hunter, or one of the guards for all she knew. With the crown gone, so was the reward.

CHAPTER 17

A silver threaded crown rested on Cassandra's temple with her hair entwined within its nooks to hold it in place. Hunter's arms were on either side of her, holding the reins close while her feet dangled on one side of the horse.

"This is rather uncomfortable," she muttered, driving her hips back slightly.

"Apparently a princess isn't supposed to be comfortable. She's supposed to look good at all times," he replied, pulling the reins so close to her stomach, she felt his knuckles brush against it and she instinctively breathed in.

"It's probably hard to imagine for you, but who would have thought you could be slowly driving me crazy with all the never-ending things you have to say that I don't need to hear."

"Sounds to me like a classic marriage already."

She twisted her head to see him. A broad smile marked the dimple in his left cheek, and she wanted to wipe the grin from his face. "I could elbow you right now."

"I'd prefer if you didn't. It would hurt me" he said matter-of-factly.

She turned her head back to face the way they were travelling. She chided, "All the more reason to do it."

"Very funny."

They came to a halt behind Queen Isla with two guards on either side of her, each on a separate horse, the hilts of their swords burning hot in the late sun.

"Why are we here?" Cassandra asked.

Hunter suspected why they were there, but he chose not to answer, shrugging his shoulders, then jumping off the horse, offering her a hand to dismount. A dark cloak hung over her shoulders like a protective shield and she followed behind him into the remains of Old Ruins.

Aylie sat in her cottage, amongst vapours and fumes from the cauldron, until Queen Isla barged through the door. She stumbled to her feet, catching the edge of the sofa to lever herself up.

"Your Majesty," she said, bowing down. "I have prepared another hundred vials for you. I was going to deliver them tomorrow at noon." The entire time, Aylie looked down at the floor, away from Queen Isla's eyes.

"Where are they?"

Aylie pointed her open palm towards two crates, upon which a few of the potted plants lay. The guards cleared them, breaking the pots on the hard floor, and lifted the crates out of the hut.

"Where are the letters? I know there are more letters. That girl walks around the kingdom like she owns the place!"

Aylie narrowed her brows, gripping her long skirt not to step on the ends. Her voice faltered, and it felt like she was inhaling too much of the fumes that seemed to be suffocating her.

"I'm not quite sure what you mean—"

"Hunter was kind enough to tell me who dared come to my castle. Apparently, a girl that did your last delivery has a close blood connection with you. But not only that. I've been told she has a presence like no ordinary Drishti. That can only mean one thing." Queen Isla paused, taking a disgusted look around the messy state of the cottage. "My question is, where are the letters? I know he wrote them. He used to write them all the time."

"You mean…" Aylie's throat closed up, unable to carry on.

"Am I not making myself clear?"

Aylie lifted her hand and pointed to a loose panel in her flooring.

"Hunter, fetch them."

After he crossed the room, taking a bundle of letters from under the floor, he held them out to Isla.

"Keep them until we're back home," she instructed.

"Now…the thing here is that we cannot risk you possibly warning the girl. As I'm sure she's as good as her father at playing this whole hide and seek charade, wouldn't you say? It would only scare her away if she suspected I was possibly looking for her."

Cassandra, standing inches behind Hunter, instinctively grabbed his forearm, digging her nails in. He heard a gasp. He unclasped her hand, whispering, "Hold it out."

Cassandra turned to leave, but her mother was quick to notice. "Where do you think you're going, dear?"

"Fresh air?" she suggested, unsure if this explanation would convince anyone, even herself.

"I demand that you stay with us. Hunter, make sure she doesn't go anywhere."

Hunter nodded sharply, stepping behind Cassandra and blocking her way from the door. She turned her head to look at him, her expression creased with worry. She then focused her eyes ahead, metres from where Aylie was standing. Out of the corner of her eye, she saw her hands grip the skirt nervously.

"Back to you…" Isla dragged the words out like a long, sickened punishment that was brewing in her mind like poison contained within the vials.

"I promise, I will not say a word." Aylie pleaded, holding her hands out in front of her, trying to protect herself from the guards that were slowly approaching her. "Not a word. Nothing. We don't even have a good relationship. She just turned up unannounced. I didn't know she would. Not a single peep. I pro—"

Aylie's mouth filled with the coppery tang of blood as the guard backhanded her cheek. A splash of brightness erupted before her vision. She moaned, doubling over and pressing her hands against the mirror on the wall behind her. It trembled and fell, crashing down by her feet, shattering into a million clear shards. A bigger piece protruded from the heap, so Aylie took the opportunity to grab a hold of it, but the second guard kicked it from her hand, bounding both of her arms behind her and twisting them so hard she winced.

"This can be as painless as you wish," said Isla. "After all, beside my potion, you've made so many other vials, it's a pity not to try one out. For good measure to see if they work as they should."

Queen Isla took a vial with cyanide in her hand, uncorking the glass with a gentle *pop*. Aylie's eyes filled with tears, biting and tossing her head back and forth. A guard stuffed his dirty fingers into her mouth, opening wide and holding her head still.

The poison swooshed in her mouth and dribbled down her chin. She fought it as hard as she could, but the liquid seeped into her throat, almost making her choke on it. She gulped down as her eyes popped out in shock. The guards threw her against the wall, and she scrambled across it, reaching the table, where her knees gave way and she crumbled down.

Cassandra looked away, her mouth falling dry as she was unable to say anything and refused to look back up, until she was led outside of the cottage by Hunter. With his strong arms, she made it back onto the horse and away from the scene. Her lips trembled. She pushed away emotions tugging at her conscience, clenching her teeth. She remained silent for the rest of the way back until she reached her bedchamber.

She threw the heavy cloak off her shoulders, letting it tumble to the floor, and attacked Hunter, her fists meeting his chest, over and over and over again.

"How could you! Why did you have to tell her? What was the reason?"

He let her hit him. With each punch, he stood stronger and taller until she gave up, walking away from him, bringing her knees up to her chest in the chair by the window. She watched as droplets of rain raced down, colliding with each other near the end.

"You didn't have to tell her anything! She wouldn't have killed anyone if you hadn't told her about that girl!" Cassandra's voice was brittle. "Do you enjoy watching all these people die?"

"There are a lot of things I do," he paused, "or have done, that you wouldn't understand."

"You said I was the same as my mother. You wanted to put all that hatred and cruelty onto my shoulders, to have someone to hate, but you're no better than her yourself! It's not me you should hate. You should hate yourself!"

His voice was warm. "You wouldn't understand, Cass." The bundle of letters was still in his coat, itching to be read. There was suddenly a note of urgency in his voice. "I'll be back soon. Keep the light on for me," he said, leaving her alone, rushing around the corner and up the spiral staircase towards Queen Isla's chamber.

Isla was already in her nightgown. Her thin and silvery braid plummeted down to her hip while she held a glass, filled with something stronger than wine by the look of its brown colour and the sound of her sigh after downing its contents, exhaling an invisible steam.

"Care to join me?" she asked.

"I need to get back to my betrothed. She's waiting," he said as a way of excusing himself, even though he knew Cassandra wanted to be left alone right now.

"I'm sure she can wait a while longer." Isla poured a second glass and pushed it into Hunter's hand. "The letters. Have you got them?"

"Yes, right here." With a smooth motion he extracted them from inside his coat, sticking his hand out to her.

"Take a drink and read them out to me," she said, her back turned to him while she circled the glass ring with her finger.

Hunter grunted, withholding his objections to the offer of a drink. He opened up one of the letters.

Dear Akela,

We have made it. Our great escape.

Away from Isla, away from the damned castle that dwells its name upon murder, upon murder, upon murder. If only our powers weren't so compelling, if only there was a way to stop the cruel reign, I would have done it, but I couldn't hurt Isla. I was unable to. I did the next best thing I thought would save you, would save us.

We have escaped and as I held you, the bundle of joy you were supposed to be, I couldn't seem to shake the feeling of something completely opposite. Not joy. Not even a smile as you wrapped your fingers around my thumb.

And I stupidly believed it was going to be the greatest feeling there ever was.

No.

All I felt was a queer, dark aura around your fair complexion and the sight of a shade of grey within your eyes, I wish wasn't there, only intensified my worries.

I had to do something.

As he read all the letters, Queen Isla failed to notice one of them was ripped in half with the second half missing that found its way deep into Hunter's boot before he entered Isla's chambers.

Hunter straightened up in his chair, throwing a glance at Isla finishing yet another one of her drinks. He gathered the letters into a pile, shuffling them neatly together.

"That's all there is, Your Majesty. Should I leave them out for you on the table?"

"No need. Burn them," she said, waving her hand at him.

He left her chamber, taking quick steps down the stairs. He sat down on the bottom one, gathering his thoughts and driving his fingers through his hair, resting them on his neck before he stood up again. The ripped page meddled his mind and he decided to call it a night, going back up to Cassandra's chamber, hoping she would be fast asleep.

"Hunter! Hunter!" An urgent call turned his head and he saw a dishevelled guard running towards him. "Hunter, we caught someone sneaking around the palace when you were gone. We've put her in the basement."

"It's late, I'll deal with it in the morning," he responded, his head clouded with the contents of the letter.

"She stole this," he gasped, pushing Cassandra's coronation crown into Hunter's hands. "She must have been in your chamber! I don't know how she sneaked past everyone. We were just outside. Someone in the market told us they saw something suspicious."

Hunter examined the crown, giving it back to the guard and telling him to return it to Princess Cassandra immediately. He then made his way to the basement; a guard outside of the cell unlocked the door, letting him in.

CHAPTER 18

The chirping sounds of crickets were stifled by the creak of the huge barn door swinging open. Ezme and Oliver's voices were audible all the way up to the thatched roof dwelling. The musty smell of manure and haystacks mixed in the air.

"Why would you even ask her for help? You knew what the answer was going to be. She is the most narcissistic, arrogant, untactful—"

"She is the only person who can help us. We can't do this on our own!" Oliver's stare intensified and Ezme's cheeks grew flustered with red patches; a heavy weight settling on her chest. "How do you expect to be able to accomplish something without suitable means and the right people for the job?"

Ezme sighed, irritated, letting the weight flutter away with her breath. "There must be another way."

"I can't think of one without Blade in on the plan."

"We need another way *without* her."

"Ez, be reasonable. Put aside the differences and name another person that's as skilful with a sharp edge as she is. If things go south, we'd want to be stuck with her and nobody else."

A creak and a quiet shuffle in the upper planks of the barn made Ezme's head swivel upward. And then a *swish*, a solitary curl of her hair trembled in the air. A dagger hit the wooden stake inches from Ezme's head. Like a shadow, Blade descended gracefully by Oliver's feet, briefly placing a hand on his shoulder to fix an uncomfortable left shoe.

"I must admit, listening to you moan about me was quite the entertainment. There were some well-sought words and I had a moment to make a list of my own too," said Blade, blowing onto her fringe to get rid of the dust that settled, while she sat above them. "My list would definitely have started with entitled and too perfect for her own good. Morally, if I were you, I'd stab myself. You constantly judge people if they don't fall into your category of 'what people should do and how they should behave'," she mimicked Ezme's voice. "You think you don't need my help, but I'd like to see you try stealing something without anyone noticing you."

"I don't think planning a murder is quite the same as some petty thievery," riposted Ezme.

"Petty," Blade contemplated, smiling. "It's charming, really. But you're right."

Ezme's brow lifted.

"You're right to think it's not the same. Because anyone can kill. It's not as much of a skill as it is to steal. Without being noticed, that is," she enunciated her words. "If I can get to someone within an arm's reach, they're as good as dead in my books. And they won't even know. But that's not why I'm here, is it?" she huffed.

Oliver leaned against the wall and smiled. Blade's sudden appearance hadn't phased him. He was used to her sneaking up on people. It sounded more like a statement than a question when he asked, "You've changed your mind?"

Ezme turned to Oliver, anger filling her lungs with fury, she deflected, "She's the last person I'd want to have on my team. See what she does? She just flings that wicked thing back and forth like it's a toy!"

"Let's cut to the chase. I have a tea scheduled at the palace. I'm not here to witness a lover's tiff, especially if I'm the subject of interest."

"This is not a lover's tiff…" She paused, trying to dampen the edge of impatience in her voice.

Blade raised her eyebrow at Oliver, sizing him up and down with a smirk. "I'm glad we have that sorted out. It's definitely good to know."

"You must be kidding me right now," Ezme spat out, walking up to Blade.

Ezme squinted, meeting a barrier she couldn't get past. She tried to concentrate again, failing at a connection with Blade that should be working.

Blade snickered, "Are you trying to summon some sort of a demon and claim my soul? Your face got all puffed up and strained. Not a pretty look."

"Why is it not working?"

Blade almost shouldered Ezme as she walked past her, removing the dagger from the post. "May I offer my humble observation? Maybe you're just a really bad sort of Drishti? Or a very rusty one? Pick whatever suits your morale better."

"Tell me why it's not working on you," Ezme demanded, inching close to her. Her hair sprang around in all directions.

"You might want to tone it down." She flicked a finger at her, pushing her back. "I could kill you before you could blink."

Ezme stormed past Oliver, but he barred her way out with his arm. "So, after all the pleasantries, can we get to work now, ladies?"

"I will kill her one day," Ezme muttered loud enough for Blade to hear.

Oliver cast Blade a look to which she turned the weapon over in between her fingers, then spoke, after taking a seat on a pile of haystacks, "I would have thought you'd known the trick, but since you don't – let me enlighten you. In this bracelet," she raised her wrist up, "is Drishti blood. Pity, it's not yours—"

"Blade," Oliver chastised her. She rolled her eyes.

Ezme furrowed her brows. Denying Blade the amusing mockery deflated the atmosphere, but she held her hand out for Ezme to take a closer look at the handmade bracelet. It was a simple design with a leather binding holding the speckle of a crystal ball. Within were pools of red and blue mixing together in twists and twirls, as if magically charmed to move in a dance only they knew the sound to.

"A cursed one can't control me while I have their blood on me," Blade explained.

The barn door flew open, pushed by Ashen's huge, furry paws. His long, silver tail circled around Ezme's feet and she crouched down to pat his head.

"It took you a while to find your true calling," Blade noted. She continued, judging from Ezme's confused expression, "Your father could do it." She flung her wrist at the wolf. "He could control those beasts."

"What changed your mind?" Oliver chimed in.

Blade smirked. "I'm sure you can figure that one out yourself."

"It's money, it's always money," Ezme spat out under her breath.

"What we need to do is use Ezme's powers. This gives us a bigger edge over Isla's control. We need to gather up more wolves and ambush the palace with their blood lusted fangs." Blade's eyes twinkled at Ashen's sharp canines.

"I'm not putting an innocent animal's life in danger. Let alone a whole pack of them," Ezme protested.

"Ez, I think we should think about this. She's right. In big enough numbers, we stand a chance," said Oliver.

"You too? When did she become the voice of reason?"

"Don't you see?" Blade asked. "Drishti will never be safe. Even if you manage to hide once or twice, they eventually find you. They find everyone. If not you, there will be others. I can simply help you achieve your goal. Good luck without me."

Blade's words wound around the space like a snake, then slowly sucked the air out. As much as Ezme hated to admit she was right, she pressed her lips together in agreement. Ashen's cool eyes rested on Blade, watching her throw the dagger up in the air, then swiftly catch it by its small hilt with precision.

Blade continued, "Our chances are better with the wolves." She met the wolf's solemn gaze and caught the blade one last time, stashing it back inside its sheath. "But first we have to prepare, rather than rely on dumb luck."

Oliver nodded, crossing his arms over his chest.

"Something strange happened yesterday," muttered Ezme, an unusual feeling tugging at her.

Oliver sat down next to Blade on top of a haystack. Ashen lain beneath his feet.

"Those guards…" Ezme paced up and down. "They were different. It felt like they weren't under anyone's compulsion. I could control them."

"That's impossible," snapped Blade.

"They wore Valeis uniforms," observed Oliver.

"I know that," said Ezme.

"So it means they are already under the Queen's compulsion," Blade stated, grabbing her dagger out again and flicking it forward like an extension of her hand.

"I know that," said Ezme. "I made a connection with one of them. And the other screamed not to look me in the eye. Now, who would do that? If they are under Isla's compulsion, then they shouldn't worry about being controlled by anyone else."

"It's impossible," said Blade, sheathing her dagger and standing up. "You couldn't have. You're probably still in shock. I get that it could have been a traumatic experience for you, but it's just not possible." Blade shook her head, crossing her arms over her chest. "When someone's under a Drishti compulsion, another Drishti cannot control them."

"That's right," Oliver agreed. "Are you sure, Ez?"

"Of course, I'm sure!" Ezme stared at Blade questioningly with an unearthed feeling she knew something, a hot shiver travelling down her spine, rolling her shoulders back. "The guard let go of a weapon right in front of me because I willed him to. I willed him to do it!"

"Could it be that she can overcome another Drishti's control?" asked Oliver, looking from Ezme to Blade.

"Impossible," she replied. "Richard couldn't and I don't suppose she could either."

"What other explanation could there be?"

Blade shrugged. "Bring one of the kids out. We can test it."

Oliver looked to Ezme for any objections, but she only nodded and left the barn. She was back a few minutes later with the oldest kid, Beckett.

Beckett squirmed and shifted from foot to foot. "I'm really not comfortable doing this to Oliver. You taught us not to use it unless it's necessary," he said to Ezme.

Ezme gathered her thoughts and placed a hand on his shoulder. He was only twelve, but almost taller than her. "This is necessary. We need to check if something's possible and we really need your help. There's no other Drishti around except for me and all of you. I chose you because you're the oldest and you've been here the longest." She took her hand off and stepped aside. "Now, can I trust you to control Oliver and break the connection when I say so?"

"Sure," he said.

The connection formed immediately when Beckett looked into Oliver's eyes. With two blinks, Beckett's silver eyes turned a hint darker, then returned back to normal.

"Make him do something funny," Blade taunted.

Beckett smirked at her with a boyish grin, ready to make things more interesting.

"Beckett, no," Ezme warned him.

"Only a little thing."

"Yes, Ezme," Blade chimed in, "only a little thing. It will be fun." Her brow quirked up in amusement and she hitched back down on the pile of hay, throwing her legs flat on top, leaning against a wooden pole.

"Oliver wouldn't appreciate it."

Blade winked at Beckett. "I'm sure he would."

Oliver walked up to Ezme and grabbed her around the waist, lifting her up. The eyes that looked back at her were not his – they felt empty. She tried to take control of him and tell him to stop spinning her around, but it didn't work.

"Put me down, Oliver," she demanded, but yet again he didn't listen. "Beckett! Down! Right now!"

Beckett obliged and soon Oliver lowered her to the ground.

"Break the connection," said Ezme. "It didn't work."

"I knew it wouldn't. It's impossible!"

"You said that about five times already."

"I think it was four times, but maybe the fifth time you will believe me when I tell you that it's *impossible*."

"We can cross that out then," said Oliver. "Thanks, Beck, but if you were going to do something funny you should have thought bigger. Maybe throwing a bucket full of water over Blade's head next time, eh?" he suggested and was met with the corners of Beckett's mouth curling up in mischief.

"You do know that wouldn't end well for you," Blade commented.

When the barn door shut after Beckett, Oliver added, "What if they weren't here on the Queen's orders? What if the uniforms they wore weren't theirs?"

"Why?" Ezme breathed out. "Why would someone do that without being in anyone's control?"

Blade snorted, "I forget how naive you can be. Not everyone's a saint like you. People do all sorts of things for many different reasons."

"For coin?" she asked.

"There's a prize for everything. I'll keep my eyes and ears open, but without a hostage, I'm unable to track them down. If I hear anything, I'll let you know," Blade said with a finality in her voice, wanting to leave the subject behind.

Ezme contemplated, "We need to do something about the children. We can't keep them in the bunker forever. They need a place to sleep."

"That's easy. We take them over to Blade's hut," Oliver suggested.

Last thing Blade wanted was to have a bunch of unknown children in her home and when she looked at Ashen it seemed as if he scowled, burrowing his face in between his paws, lolling his tongue out almost in blatant mockery.

Blade deflected, "I have acquaintances in Zeffari's Keep that could look after them."

"No," Oliver protested. "In times like this we can't trust anyone. Fools do worse things for coin."

"I know a few people that would never—"

"No," Ezme agreed. "I'm with Oliver on that one. We can't trust anyone else for the sake of the children."

Blade gave up. "Gather them up. I'll be back in an hour with a few more horses."

Before the sun fell and twinkling sparks welcomed the sky, Blade was riding horseback with Beckett. Victor was leading the carriage Oliver had borrowed from his friend along with Quinto, Ember, Khari and Liya while Oliver rode with Adie behind Ezme and Emilia.

"I'm tired of running," Adie yawned, laying his head down on the horse's neck, watching the moving trees blur into one big splodge in his vision.

"We all are," Oliver responded, trailing slowly behind Ezme.

He watched as her hair plopped up and down with the motion of the horse. She looked over her shoulder and his eyes darted to hers, seeing them so clearly despite the darkening sky. He smiled at her, hoping to lighten the burden she carried, but instead, her face deepened with an unspoken concern. With agonising pain, she turned away, biting the inside of her cheek, secretly wanting to turn back again and smile, but choosing not to.

CHAPTER 19

Everyone gathered behind Blade's hut around the barren, hollow space, large enough for a fire pit. Oliver started a feeble smoke and soon the pit engulfed sticks and branches with dried leaves, collected by Victor with the children's help hours before, giving a warm ambiance to the darkness that was setting around them.

Blade's hair flowed with a fiery spark while Ezme's curls turned and twisted around her cheeks, darkening her skin. At first, Blade sat down atop the edge of the bark, but with time, she scuttled closer to Ezme, sharpening the ends of a bunch of sticks with her dagger. Ezme passed a wicker basket with chestnuts around, helping Emilia, Quinto, Liya and Ember nail one each onto the sticks while Khari and Beckett insisted on doing it themselves.

"Wine anyone?" Oliver asked, holding out a wineskin.

"I'll have a sip," Ezme responded, catching it with both hands, unscrewing the cap and tasting the aromatic liquid fill her throat in a pleasant trickling sensation, sloshing down and warming her up.

Blade watched as the chestnut on her stick started to roast, cracking its hard skin, before asking, "So, who here has played Never Have I Ever before?"

"Blade," Ezme protested, but Blade just held out her hand to silence the objections.

Adie's head immediately perked up, interested, and he stopped fiddling with the stick over the crackling fire. "What's that?"

"It's a game where you say something you have never done before and whoever has done it raises their hand. For example, never have I ever sat at a bonfire and whoever has done it will raise their hand."

"I've never done it," Emilia said, keeping her hands on her knees while Oliver took care of roasting both of their chestnuts; a stick in each hand. "Uh, I know! Never have I ever not listened to Victor!"

Victor grumbled and shifted in his seat an inch forward, shaking his head, however, a sly smile slid across his lips unnoticed. Everyone amongst the children kept their hands on their laps while Ezme raised her hand up in the air to which Emilia shot her a surprised glance.

"Hey! Put your hand up!" Ezme urged Oliver.

He laughed, shrugging his shoulders. "I can't, my hands are full."

"That's just not fair, is it?"

"It is not to say that any of you are allowed to not listen to me," Victor proclaimed in his deep voice, twisting his stick over the flames.

Oliver looked between Khari and Beckett as they tried to ignore the question; Khari averted her eyes to the sky while Beckett's chestnut fell into the fire and he poked at it with the sharp end of the stick.

"That's right. You don't want to mess with Victor," Oliver chuckled, baring his teeth.

The smell of a crackling bonfire started to sink through their clothes. Their faces lit like the stars in the night sky as questions circled one after the other.

Something about the flames rendered them content, almost nostalgic, at how quickly the wood was turning black and soon falling dead into ashes. But for those unspoken moments, the fire offered just the right amount of warmth everyone needed to feel better.

"Right," Victor got up, clapping his hands on his thighs. "Time to sleep, everyone."

"What about a goodnight story?" Emilia objected, pouting.

"It's very late," Ezme began.

"It was a cold and dark night. Just like tonight," Blade said, ignoring Ezme again, staring into the darkened petals of ashes swooning under the barest touches of air. "A princess named Ezme lived among many trees with a pet squirrel on her arm."

Few of the children laughed. Oliver tried to hold off a burst of laughter, almost snorting, when Ezme shot him a glance, crossing her arms. Adie shuffled closer to the pit, closer to Blade, leaning his back against the fallen bark. He drew his knees up to his chest, plonking his head onto them.

Beckett turned his attention partly to poking the dying flame, trying to stir it back to life, while Khari and Ember also neared closer to Blade. Only Quinto seemed uninterested in the story, staring far into the horizon, far above the mountains where a shadow of an eagle or a hawk flew in circles. Liya followed Victor into the hut to help him set the sleeping spaces for everyone.

"It wasn't a regular squirrel. It could fly. Soar high above the trees and bring Ezme news of the upcoming danger. Once, the squirrel scouted the sky to see a dark and hooded figure forcing its way through to the cabin the princess lived in and hurried along to bring the word to Ezme. But guess what?"

"What?" Khari asked.

"Ezme was asleep and the squirrel couldn't get into the house."

"Why?" Ember asked.

"Because all the windows were closed and even though the squirrel could fly, it could not open doors."

"That is ridiculous," Ezme said, getting up and following Victor and Liya into the hut to help them prepare beds for everyone.

"I quite like it," Oliver laughed, holding a half-asleep Emilia on his lap, to which she dragged her fists across her eyes.

"What happened to the squirrel?" she yawned.

"The squirrel gathered up all the other squirrels it knew and flew all around the dark figure that was coming for Ezme. The squirrels were her friends and wanted to protect her."

"This doesn't make any sense," Beckett mocked.

"Course it does," Blade answered quickly. "You just have to look for the hidden meaning. Not everything is given to you on a platter."

"But Ezme doesn't have any squirrels and she's not a princess," Emilia protested, tilting her head to see into the hut to look at Ezme through the cloud of smoke in between them.

"I think what Blade is trying to say is that Ezme's squirrels were her friends and they would do anything to protect her as they loved her," Oliver pondered for a moment, scooping Emilia up in his arms. She tangled her arms around his neck.

"Are we the squirrels?" Adie asked.

"I'm no squirrel," Beckett said, throwing the stick into the now dead fire.

"I think it's time to sleep now." Oliver walked through the door, laying Emilia under a blanket and gathering everyone else to sleep on the floor. Everyone but Adie followed as if on command.

"This story is not very convincing," he said to Blade.

"I'm not very good at telling happy-ending stories," she said. "Go to bed, kid."

"Only if you tell me a real story. Squirrels don't fly and happy endings don't happen often. I know that much."

"Well, aren't you a smart kid?" She got up and ushered Adie inside. "Tell you what. I could tell you a better story tomorrow morning if you want to help me hunt game for dinner."

Adie's eyes lit up and he failed to contain a smile. "I'll be the first one up," he promised, running over to the last unoccupied blanket on the floor.

"Just don't wake me up before everyone else is awake, kid," she replied, untying the shawl from around her neck and dropping it over the sofa, where she was going to sleep herself.

"I forgot to check on the horses," Victor remembered.

"It's okay, I'll check on them," Blade offered, feeling the chill sweep across her neck as she opened the door again.

Above the fire pit, grey melted into black sparks and everything felt suspended in the air, absolutely still, the moment Blade's eyes fell upon the one person she wished never to see again.

CHAPTER 20

The moon didn't reflect in calming waves off her glaring hair. Instead, it oozed in suffocating dark circles. The cascading fire cast his shadow like a black veil over rough charcoal stones.

Blade's eyes met Nathe's expectantly, searching for an explanation within. His trousers were dirty with flecks of dried paint all over and his hand moved towards her but ended up shooting upward to rest on the back of his neck. He wet his bottom lip, filled with nervous anticipation of Blade's reaction.

"You skiving little piece..." she hushed her voice, shutting the door to the hut behind her and crossing the distance between them.

As she reached for the dagger at her hip, her burning red hair tangled with leaves and dirt with a sudden gust of erratic wind from the tree above.

Nathe's fingers immediately wound tight around her wrist, forcing the blade to fall from her grip. He slid his palm onto her waist and pulled her close, so their bodies collided. He inched his head lower, unable to take his eyes from her shocked, parted lips. Her heavy, unequal breath caressed the hollow of his neck.

She pulled back, but he remained holding her for a moment longer. Her eyes searched for something known, but all she saw was sorrow and her brow furrowed.

"I haven't done anything," he snapped and let go of her small figure. As a result, she staggered backward, creating an impenetrable wedge between them, filled with unsaid words, itching to escape.

She watched him pick her dagger up from the floor and his eyes focused on the edge finish, sliding his forefinger against it to the point it drew his blood.

"You stabbed me in the back," she said. "You orchestrated the whole thing so that Hunter could manipulate me into helping him."

"I didn't," he denied, his head low on his shoulders.

"Then who did if not you? Who? You're the one that stuck this stupid piece of paper in my pocket." She reached within her coat to pull out the drawing. Crunching it in her hand, she aimed it at his chest. "You're the one that told me there was a prize for the stupid crown. You did this to me! You made me get caught!" Her eyes ignited even more and her jaw clenched.

"Well, maybe you deserved to know how it felt to be abandoned by the ones you thought cared for you. To rely on someone, only to find out it was all a lie. What they shared, what they had." He chucked the dagger up in the air and she caught it, holding it firmly by her side. "Hurts, doesn't it? To be lied to? By me?"

"How could you have trusted Hunter? He could have killed me if he wanted to! I would never have hurt you like this."

She turned to leave, but as she walked towards the back of the hut to tend to the horses, he added, "Oh, but you did. You did. You hurt me more than any physical pain could."

"I had to," she muttered, holding back the tension to seep from her shoulders onto her tingling shade of flushed cheeks, swallowing a hard breath. "I left so you could survive. I left for your sake. To save your life," she spat the words onto the ground, her back to him.

His steps drew near and she could feel him close to her. A tiny breath away. He reached for her wrist and twisted her to face him, her back meeting the wooden gate of the horse's enclosure, eyes looking up to meet his hardened, full of pain stare.

"There were other choices to make. You could have chosen me over whatever you thought was best."

His hand slowly caressed her cheek and she let herself forget for a moment why she left all those years back. His touch felt right, it felt like it belonged.

"I had no choice!" She pushed him with both her hands. "Hunter warned me they would kill you if I stayed. I left you a note. I told you to leave, to run as far as you could and never look back."

She could still feel his touch on her wrist, the closeness she longed for. But she had to push those weak feelings away the moment she felt herself melt in his arms. She had to be stronger. She had always been stronger. Always, but never with him.

"But you never listen, do you? You had to stick around. You're lucky to be alive – especially since Hunter knows where you are!"

"I can take care of myself. You never had to do that for me."

"I needed to. You would have died. He said—"

"Maybe I'd rather die in a warm bed where you laid with me, instead of suddenly waking up and seeing you were gone!"

"Don't be so sentimental. Feelings pass. It's just a matter of time."

"I loved you," he said. "But now I think you're just a cruel bitch who only cares for herself."

"Don't…" She shook her head. "Don't you dare talk to me like this." Her lips quivered and she stared at him intensely until something in her chest snapped and pulled her towards him.

In less than three quick steps she was inching up on her toes with her entwined hands at the back of his neck, pulling him towards her mouth, but she hesitated an inch before his lips. His hair was long enough for her to grab it and pull away again.

"I must go," she said.

His reply was less than a whisper, "Don't. Not again."

"Nathe, don't do this," she breathed out. "Why can't you just let me be?"

His hand shot up to pick something from her hair, but he paused when she eyed him with a question. "You have a, um…leaf," he offered as an explanation.

Her fingers slid down the strands, grabbing the leaf and crunching it in her hand, letting its remnants fall to her feet.

"What Oren did was not my fault. Hunter paid him off," he explained. "If I knew he would do something like that, I would never have even suggested for you to go anywhere near him. And the crown…it was all a set up too.

"It was Ava. She was in contact with Hunter. I didn't know until last night. I came here as soon as I found out what she'd done. I was hoping you had managed to get out of there without a scratch. You always do."

Blade unlatched the gate and ran her fingers through her horse's mane. "I don't want to see you. Go away, Nathe."

Though at the mention of his name, her voice unknowingly softened, giving him enough of a weapon to linger. Before he managed to say anything else, she quickly added, her voice roughening up, "I'd rather you go away."

"Don't do this."

"Do what?"

"Shut me out."

"You think seeing you is easy? It's not," she snapped, walking in between other horses to check on them before returning outside of the gate, where Nathe's arms held it down, not letting her leave.

"Do you really want me to leave? And never come back again?" he asked.

"Yes," she said, looking into his eyes.

"You're lying."

"It's easier that way."

"I never would have thought you'd be the one to take an easy way out. Not now. Not ever."

The ends of her hair brushed her shoulders when she shook her head. "Nathe, I can't, we've been down this road. My presence is not something you should consider as safe."

"Meet with me in three days. Meet with me where we first met. Can you do that?"

"I don't remember where—"

"You do. You remember perfectly well where. In three days at noon."

She stared at him, stoic as always, her lips pursed.

"Just nod you'll be there."

She shook her head. "Nathe..."

The smoke in the fire pit stopped swaying in the air by the time she returned to the hut, closing the door behind her quietly. Except for soft turning and deep breaths, the hut was silent. Still and asleep. She noticed Adie was curled up to the wall, as far away from everyone else as possible.

"Are you okay?" Oliver muttered with one eye opened while he rubbed the other one, then yawned.

"Go back to sleep," she said with the intention of making herself comfortable on the sofa, but her feet led her outside to see Nathe mount his horse.

"Nathe!"

He turned the horse around, looking down on her.

"Come inside. You can't ride at night."

She didn't fail to see a smile on his face when he said, "You once told me riding at night was the best time to ride a horse."

"Come inside," she insisted, leaving the door open for him.

CHAPTER 21

Adie was up for the best part of an hour. An early rustle of leaves dusting the barren earth around the crooked hut and a lonely chirrup of a lost bird were the only sounds, apart from Adie's eager footsteps.

Emilia asked through a yawn, "Why are you awake?

"I'm going hunting," he said excitedly.

She turned onto her other side and placed a pillow over her head to dull out his small feet marching relentlessly up and down the room, careful not to stomp on anyone.

Oliver opened his eyes too, staring at Ezme's hair, curling in honey-soaked rays on the floor, bouncing down the side of her shoulder. A blanket covered half of her body, while her feet were hidden in the underbelly of the sofa Nathe was sleeping on, crammed with Blade on the opposite end.

He observed Ezme for a minute while Blade threw the blanket off and shuffled around the kitchen, mixing coffee beans with a fresh mug of water, impatiently holding it over a small fire, almost burning her fingers. Adie was by her side, stomping from one foot to the other, pleased with himself after Blade rolled off the sofa after nudging her ten times, if not more.

Blade stifled a yawn, pushing Adie away from her with her foot after she jumped up onto the tabletop, gulping down the last drops of coffee and muttering under her breath something about an ungodly hour.

She finally jumped down, manoeuvring in between a floor full of snuggled up bodies, picking up her coat and reaching into the pocket. Her eyes found Oliver's as her fingertips felt the rough edge of a crumpled parchment, remembering what Hunter had given her.

She had forgotten all about it after the eventful day, not to mention the encounter with Nathe, who muddled her thoughts once again as he shuffled to face the back of the sofa. Blade inched closer and covered his shoulders with the blanket she had been sleeping under.

"Hold this," she said, extending a pocketknife to Adie. Delicately, he held it with two hands, careful not to drop it, as it felt a little heavy. "It's a knife for heaven's sake, kid, not a dead pigeon."

Adie's grip strengthened on the knife's hilt and he gave Blade a sharp nod, swallowing his embarrassment.

"I'll be a moment. Fill some pouches with water and after you're done, pack a bag for us. Wait here until I return."

Blade diverted her eyes back to Oliver and, with a jerk of her head, made him follow her outside, closing the door behind them, making sure Ezme was still deep in her dreams.

"What is it? It's freezing out here," Oliver moaned, running his palms over his shoulders, up and down, to create a flicker of warmth, but his attempts were futile with the morning breeze sweeping his breath in an icy parlour.

"I think we need to pay Ezme's mother a visit. I'm in possession of two letters I feel you should read."

Oliver creased his brows sceptically. "How did you get them in the first place is my question?"

"I had business to take care of and a friend of mine happened upon them."

Oliver sized her up and down sceptically. "A friend?"

"That's completely irrelevant. Why don't you hurry up and read them before everyone wakes up?" she urged him. "I thought you should know what's in there."

He grabbed the letter, turning it the right way up and began reading.

Dear Akela,

I did what I had to do.

We were in the woods, running from the ghosts of my past, from Isla, and each day you got bigger and bigger until the moment you called me "papa". Two syllables, two identical sounds. If you think about it, it's just a word.

The moment I heard it for the first time, and it pains me to admit this, I wished you hadn't said it. I didn't want you to grow used to me, I didn't want you to love me when I knew we weren't going to stay together.

We had to separate. For your own good.

I watched as a huge elm tree caught your attention and your eyes began to climb its branches, until they reached the peak and you watched the clouds move soundlessly across the azure blue sky. I turned my back for only a moment, leaving you on the soft grass to wander on all fours.

It was a second. Perhaps even less than that. When I turned back, my heart jumped out of my chest at what I saw, yet I wasn't surprised.

There was a wolf right in front of you and your hand reached out to its ear, pulling at it. The wolf only weaved its tail around you to make sure you were warm and rested his head on the damp grass. I searched and saw a hill with huge stones covering the entrance to something that looked like a cave. You rolled on your stomach, still tugging at the poor wolf's ear.

When I reached out to you, the wolf first bared his teeth at me, but then relaxed his jaw and let me pick you up in my arms. I saw in the reflection of his eyes that you took control of him and, naturally, when I tried to claim him under my own compulsion, I couldn't.

Then I saw his eyes falter in colour, flicking briefly light to dark, and I understood in that moment, when the wolf perked up, lowering his snout to the ground, showing us his deadly canines, he was ready to pounce and make us his dinner.

You released him from your control, looking at me with your big grey eyes and trying to pull a button from my shirt.

Cautiously, I stepped back, forcing the wolf to look into my eyes so I could now take control of him to make sure he didn't hurt us.

I knew I had this gift since a very young age. Perhaps it was the reason why I was a good farmer. Animals did exactly what I willed them to. At the end of the day it was easy work, easy money. But I never, until now, kept an animal to stay by my side.

Since the incident, the wolf had always been close to me, watching over us when we slept at night. I found comfort in knowing he was there.

Until I finally plucked the courage to visit Aylie. The herbalist I heard about who practiced darker kinds of magic. It was time for us to separate.

Blade leaned over the corner of the hut to sneak a peek inside through the window.

"Keep reading," she said, after checking Ezme was still asleep.

Oliver turned the page over to another entry.

Dear Akela,

If you were here, you would have known you have a sister now. Aylie and I named her Ezme. Wherever you are in the world, I want you to know I love you and never stopped loving you. You need to understand this was for the best. Ezme would love you too if you ever met each other.

Maybe, down the line, you will and maybe, down the line, we would live to see the day when peace is restored to our kingdom. Until then, stay hidden. And take care of yourself. You're stronger than you think.

Oliver swallowed. It took him a while to comprehend what he had read, handing the letters back to Blade, who stashed them quickly away.

"Ezme...*My* Ezme?" he asked.

"Yes," Blade nodded, crossing her arms and pacing up and down.

"So that means..."

"It means Richard wrote those letters. It means Richard had two daughters of which one he gave up."

Oliver's mind raced, running through the information he gathered in such a short space of time. Trying to find a logical order.

He said, "If this is true, it means Akela is not only the daughter of Richard but of Queen Isla too. There is an heir out there, older, older and more legitimate than Princess Cassandra."

"It appears that way, but what interests me is what Richard did with her."

"I wonder where she is now. Does she know? Is she alive? We have to tell Ezme she has a half-sister. We have to find Akela."

"No," Blade said sharply. "Ezme can't know. At least not yet. We need her to focus and not get distracted.

Without her, our chances at getting to Isla and breaking her defences are weak, close to none."

Something rattled inside the hut and then a quiet 'sorry' escaped Adie's mouth. Blade saw Victor get up from the floor, helping Adie mop up the water that spilled.

"Where did you get these letters from?" Oliver asked.

"It doesn't matter. What matters is that we don't have the whole story. We still don't know what happened with Akela. And I suspect me having access to those letters means Queen Isla might know about Richard's second child too. If she knows, she will most likely go after Ezme. We must be the first to strike. Knowing Isla's weakness, what she's after, makes her vulnerable." Blade grabbed Oliver by his elbows. "Come with me to Old Ruins. Maybe there are more letters. Maybe Aylie knows a lot more than she lets on."

"What about Ezme?"

"She stays here. She's safe for the time being. I don't think Isla would be venturing out days before Cassandra's coronation to find Ezme. Let's go tomorrow morning."

Oliver rubbed his eyes, debating what the right course of action was – if lying to Ezme was a good idea.

"You know she will freak out. We don't have the time for her to come to terms with her father leading a life she had no idea about. I need you to promise you won't tell her anything. And I need you to come with me to follow all the leads we have," Blade prompted him, twisting her head over her shoulder to check what was happening inside.

"Fine," he said. "But what will we say?"

"For such a clever man, you can be so daft sometimes." She buttoned up her coat, stuffing the tunic inside her trousers. She continued, "You're a healer, Oliver. People need you. That's enough of an explanation to go and do some good. I happen to know you usually do rounds around the village once a week. I'm sure there's work for you to be had."

"With Esteracre burning down, I wasn't going to. I was going to stay with Ezme and the children."

"They have her and Victor. It's enough. It's a lie for the greater good. People lie all the time. Get used to it."

Blade tapped on the window with her knuckles and Adie ran outside with a rucksack full of what he deemed necessary survival elements for their hunting trip out into the unknown.

"You have enough stuff there, kid?" she asked.

"I have everything we need," he said, smiling.

"You're okay to carry it? 'Cause I for sure won't be carrying all of this once you get tired."

He nodded, shouldering the bag that was almost his size.

"Let's go, we have rabbits to hunt," she said, setting out towards the depths of the base of the mountains some distance from the hut. "Oliver!" she shouted.

He turned, resting his hand on the doorframe. "What?"

She hadn't looked back when she said, "Tell Nathe to go away."

"Sure, I'll do just that," he muttered under his breath, watching as Blade's home came to life, becoming chaos, just like in a beehive.

"Where are we going?" Adie tried to keep up with Blade, walking closely behind her.

"Hunting," she replied.

"But where? Over there? High in the mountains?"

"No."

"Is it far where we're going? Are we going to stop soon?"

She kept her ears and eyes open as they walked in the outstretched hollow of rocks beneath their shoes. All they could hear were their breaths and steps. "We just left, kid."

"I packed a blanket in case we want to—"

"Shh," she urged, stopping abruptly and holding out a hand to Adie's mouth.

Blade's dagger cut through the raw morning air reaching the throat of a small animal hopping from rock to rock in a fast and clean death. Adie gasped, both horrified and impressed at the way Blade wielded her weapon by the mere sound of an animal in the distance.

"How did you—" his mouth almost formed an 'o' and he blinked a few times, watching her pick the rabbit by its ears and throw it into the bag Adie was carrying.

"By not talking and paying attention to my surroundings. Give it a try," she said.

Each step they took left a fresh footprint in the snow as they ventured further into the mountains, finding a peaceful, secluded place covered in a white flutter. The bushes were swaying and the tracks of a goat or a stray deer were the only marks around. Small prints behind one of the bushes caught Adie's attention. He stretched his hand out, wanting to pass through the branches to the other side to follow them, but he quickly recovered it, hissing and stepping away, finding out its leaves were prickly.

"Prints!" he told Blade.

"Where's that small knife I gave you?"

He quickly reached into his pocket, clumsily turning it the right way up. "Can I kill something now?"

Blade almost chuckled. "First, you really need to lower your voice, otherwise you'll scare every animal away," she whispered, crouching down by him.

She took the bag off his shoulders, leaving it on the ground. She clasped her fingers around his small wrist, making sure he was holding the weapon correctly.

"Look," a soft, almost inaudible whisper made Adie focus on a family of rabbits.

"You want to pull your wrist back and snap, releasing it at the right moment. Observe closely where you want the blade to land and guide your release with your instinct. Measured breaths, Adie. Don't hold it," she said his name for the first time and Adie wanted to smile, expanding his chest.

He withdrew his hand, a furrow appearing on his forehead. "They're a family," he said, "I don't want to kill a family."

"It's very cold out here. They won't survive long. If we don't kill them and feed everyone back home, a bear or a wolf will come along and eat them. It's either or. It's the circle of life."

"That circle sucks," Adie whimpered, twisting his mouth into a disapproving snarl.

"I'm afraid life is not fair sometimes," she agreed, the corner of her mouth lifting up to form a grin, shaking her head.

She flicked Adie's wrist towards the rabbits, quickly pulling two more daggers from her belt, and in quick succession, killed the remaining two. She turned to him, dragging his chin with her finger to face her.

"Listen, you're a good kid. But one thing you have to learn from me is to take care of yourself," she said. After a moment, she added, "And I suppose others too. People you care for. You sometimes have to do what is required of you to survive and help others survive."

"I guess so." He wiggled his foot in the snow, mixing the white powder with dirty gravel underneath. Good mixed with bad. There wasn't good without the bad and bad without the good. "You said last night you would tell me a story. A real story."

"I did, didn't I? But come to think of it…" Adie's eyes were glued to Blade's, waiting. "Real stories aren't told, kid. They're lived."

Before turning to look at the dead animals, Adie considered Blade's words with a glower on his face. He said, "Let's get them."

"Not that they'll hop away now," Blade mused.

CHAPTER 22

Following Ashen's furry tail, Ezme wandered into a grove of trees a mile from the crooked hut. She flicked the branches away and squeezed in between the bare, narrow trees while her boots crunched on the leaves beneath. A cold gust of wind ruffled her hair into a bigger mess than it already was, and she zipped her coat all the way up, scrunching Oliver's hat on top of her head.

She picked up a pinecone and stood still for a while, turning it in between her frozen fingers. Then, with all the strength she could muster, she threw it as far and as hard as she could in front of her. Hot, prickling tears neared in the hollows of her eyes, ready to pour down, but she bit the inside of her cheek, stopping her bottom lip from quivering and taking a deep breath in.

"From my first steps to your last," she whispered, outlining the half-key necklace with her fingers, gathering a flicker of warmth inside of her with the thought of her father.

A ray of sunshine protruded between oak trees, catching her face and bringing her attention to a squirrel climbing up the bark. She momentarily closed her eyes, letting the sun catch her skin in a muster of a delicate touch. She let out a long breath, opening her eyes and tucking the necklace back underneath her blouse.

A couple trees away, Ashen twisted his neck sideways, letting a gloved hand slide from the top of his head down to his back. He extended his paws under Blade's touch.

Black leather boots reached up to her knees, beige trousers tied with a string at the top. Her top was creased, once white, now dirty grey, washed too many times by hand. Ezme marched past Blade without a word.

"Stop spying on me," she barked, tapping her thigh for Ashen to come to her side.

Blade kept a firm distance, her movements as quiet as a faltering leaf on a branch, following her. "Not my fault Oliver is worried about you."

An edge of impatience crept into her voice and she tried to dampen it. "I don't need a babysitter."

Ashen lowered his nose to the ground and his ears shot up in alert. In between the trees, a thin beam of light cut right before his paws and his eyes turned into a narrow sliver. He began growling.

"What is it, Ashen?" Ezme asked, noticing a rush of air striking her cheeks as the tremble of the ground shook the leaves.

Blade instinctively crouched down, reaching with one hand for the dagger wrapped around her calf and with the other hand for the blade at her belt. The leather binding unfastening in less than the blink of an eye. A pack of five wolves circled them, all growling louder and louder the closer they came.

Ezme's hand flew up, catching Blade's gaze over her shoulder, "Don't. Don't do anything."

"Are you out of your mind? I don't fancy being their snack!"

"Do *not* hurt them, Blade. Give me a moment," she insisted.

Ashen followed Ezme like a faithful shadow as she stepped forward. She flicked the hair that swept onto her cheeks behind her. She searched the depths of hostile stares until she spotted the biggest wolf out of the pack. An alpha male. Angry bile plopping down from his muzzle by the ready-to-attack claws, cupping the ground.

One wolf, two wolves, three, four and five...

Ezme took each in turn until all five of the wolves were under her compulsion; their teeth unclenching along with death rippling claws retracting beneath. Blade sheathed her weapons, wearily stomping on the ground around the wolves with her eyes narrowing at their every movement.

"Relax," said Ezme. "They'll behave now."

"I trust that they're in control, but it doesn't change the fact they're under *your* control and we aren't exactly on the best of terms."

If it were anyone else, Ezme might have believed that the words were said with a hint of jealousy, but she brushed that thought away as quickly as it occurred.

"I won't set them on you if that's what you're thinking."

Blade gave a sharp nod, rolling her shoulder back into a straight stance, muttering, "You better not."

All of the wolves curled up by Ezme's feet, resting their heads on the ground in an act of obedience, except Ashen whose wet nose wiggled its way into Blade's palm, and she stroked his mane from the top of his head to his neck.

Blade's eyes ignited with a hopeful light, a half smirk painting her face. "We've got ourselves a little army."

Ezme winced, also giving one of the wolves a stroke through its thick, dirty mane.

"We have to use them." Blade turned her attention from Ashen to Ezme.

"I know," she sighed. "But what if they get hurt? I don't want them to get hurt."

Blade could have said anything. She could have reasoned it was better for a blasted animal that would have torn them apart without a second glance to die than any more Drishti. She could have said anything to persuade Ezme this was the right course of action by using wolves against humans. Wolves were much stronger than humans and with the right numbers, they could have a shot at overthrowing Isla's rule.

Instead, all she said was, "Oliver will be there to lick their wounds if anything happens."

Ezme gathered herself up and with a finality in her voice, she decided, "Help me train them."

"There's an open field not far from here," Blade said, jutting her chin in the direction away from the mountains where Ezme was initially heading. "Let's get to work."

Ashen trod on the sodden mud, splashing it against tree barks as he ran from one end of the field to the other, quickly avoiding a narrow set of trees in a curved path along the stream. A trickle that started up in the mountains, flowed all the way south past Blade's crooked hut, Zeffari's Keep and Esteracre woods where it swirled further east.

"I'm seeing a lot of quick, but not a lot of quiet. They need to be quiet. Quick but quiet."

"I'm trying!" Ezme wallowed in defence.

"Try harder. They're born predators with a killer instinct. All they lack is a little control and grace to be more deadly."

"Teaching a wolf to be graceful is like teaching you about manners," Ezme mimicked silently to herself, twisting her mouth into a snarl.

"What was that?" Blade raised an eyebrow, turning to face Ezme.

"Nothing."

"You have a gift like nobody else. Use it. Use it better."

Ezme's oversized jumper sleeves fell down to her elbows as she reached up to tie her hair back into a high knot. As she flicked her hands back down, her thumb caught the string of a necklace resting below the hollow of her neck, bringing it over the front of her clothes.

Blade's eyes fixed on the half-broken key. She frowned as she scanned its rusty ridges. "Where did you get that?"

"Father gave it to me when he…" She didn't have to finish the sentence.

Blade nodded thoughtfully and averted her eyes towards the field, watching the wolves prowl around. "I'm sorry for your loss."

In a fleeting moment, Ezme wanted to reach out to Blade and give her a hug. There was a certain wobble to her words as she offered her condolences, despite not knowing Richard well.

"Are you okay?" Ezme dared to ask, inches away to lay a friendly hand on Blade's back. She quickly withdrew it when Blade crouched down to sit on the grass, crossing her legs.

"Why wouldn't I be?"

Ezme joined her after brushing away pebbles and drawing her knees up to her chest, resting her forearms on top.

"Nathe left this morning and I thought—"

"Whatever you thought, keep it to yourself. Run Ashen again."

Ezme's shoulders hunched. She made all the wolves lay down while she focused on Ashen making the trail around the trees, down and up the rocks once more. His paws were heavy on the ground and the growl within his throat escaped a few times. She made him do it again, and again.

After a third attempt, Ashen's paws seemed to have gotten lighter and, except for the brush of his tail against the tree barks, the growls had disappeared too.

"Have you ever had anyone under your compulsion before?

Ezme didn't answer.

"You haven't? If I had your powers—"

"Well, you don't, so don't say what you would or wouldn't have done. We're quite different and I think we established that a long time ago."

"I didn't mean to strike a nerve there," Blade smirked. "I'm just saying, the more you use your powers the better you get."

"Nathe?" It was a statement more than a question. Blade knew a lot about Drishti because Nathe was one of them too. Ezme added, tilting her head, "I saw the look on your face when he was there."

"This shouldn't concern you. We need you to control the wolves, so we can do our job properly. Last thing I want is a hiccup inside the castle."

Ezme didn't give up. "I saw in your eyes there was history there. Something almost untouchable."

"Spare me your analysis. Don't act like you're an expert on everything when you don't even know how to handle Oliver yourself."

"Handle Oliver?" Ezme's brow flicked up. "Oliver doesn't need to be handled."

"That boy is completely in love with you and all you do is push him away," Blade bit back and, as soon as she said it, the words hit close to home.

It sounded almost ironic because that was exactly what she had been doing with Nathe. Although in her defence, she had a reason. She was protecting him.

"He's not in love with me," Ezme snorted, her voice higher than usual. "He can't be. We kissed once, but it was just that. A little kiss. I don't think he can be in love with me. Surely—"

"You're blabbering…and I'm starting to question if you're the right person to overthrow the Queen."

"My romantic life has nothing to do with the ability to lead a pack of wolves. Oliver and I are complicated."

"And it seems to me that you and the wolves are complicated too. Forget me. Forget Nathe. *That* is a complicated situation, yours isn't. And don't ask questions because I won't tell you about it. But come to think of it, we're actually more alike than you think."

"I'm nothing like you," she quipped.

"That's flattering, thank you. Now, listen. You try to hide it, but you're just as stubborn as I am and quite frankly, you're even worse at showing your hand when it matters. If you don't do something, you're just going to push him further away.

"Honestly, I'm still appalled at how this is taking you both so long. It's only natural. The amount of time you two spend together, I'm shocked you're not married yet."

"Are you done?" Ezme asked. "I have some training to do. I'd appreciate it if you were quiet."

Blade shook her head low on her shoulders. "Go ahead. Run them again."

CHAPTER 23

The door to Aylie's cottage was open.

Blade's nose wrinkled in disgust at the smell inside, despite the sweet undertone of dying daffodils on the windowsill. Oliver waded over broken glass crunching under his boots to reach Aylie's side, grabbing her wrist and checking her pulse.

He observed the struggle that happened around her as she lay surrounded by pieces of shiny glass from the mirror, its frame kicked to the side of the room. She looked almost peaceful, except for the purple, bruised rings around her wrists and higher up by her elbows.

Whatever was cooking in the huge cauldron in the middle of the room spilled over the brim and trickled in all directions, creating a puddle so heavy it extinguished the fire underneath it.

Blade pursed her lips, pushing all the windows wide open to help rid of the stench of a dead body. Not to mention horrific smells of everything mixing in the air, from the leaky cauldron to herbs in potted grounds, decaying flowers scattered in every visible place and uncorked vials of different mixtures.

"So much for finding out more," Blade hissed, disappointment seeping onto her tongue.

"Show some respect," said Oliver.

She wedged open a crack in the floorboards, booting it away. "For the dead? The dead are better off than we are."

Her fingers zoomed into the dark hole, searching for something to grip. When she withdrew her hand, it was full of cobwebs. She cursed under her breath, then got down on her knees to see if there was anything she was missing, tucked away in a corner. She almost caught her hand on a nail that was sticking out beneath.

She pushed herself up and left Aylie's cottage to catch a fresh breath outside. Oliver walked up to Aylie, motionless on the floor, covered her head with a blanket, then pocketed a few vials of poison from the crate, closing the door behind him.

An eerie, screeching sound reverberated in their ears and before Blade could see what it was, she threw a dagger at the base of the door, catching the furry part of a tail. The cat whisked its teeth at her and scratched on the gravel, ready to pounce in attack or defence. Blade stomped her foot and the cat jostled in between Oliver's legs, speeding off into the distance, his tail wagging behind in a haze.

The Old Ruins were just as their name proclaimed. Roofless, windowless concrete ruins. Worn down by rain, snow and wind. The occasional stones were mossy and parched with a feeble sun exposing their cracks.

Blade kicked the frame of the door and with a painful yelp, bit her bottom lip. The wood cracked away easily, leaving a hole. She wiggled her boot out of the hole. The black hairband loosened on her head and she tied it up, bringing her hair under the collar of her coat.

"Oliver, come here, quick!" she called.

Faint imprints of hooves caught his attention. "Should we follow—"

Blade stormed past without a word, mounting the horse and tracking the prints ahead. It was obvious to Blade who was responsible for the mess in the cottage and subsequently, Aylie's death. She swatted a branch away as the horse sped through the open outstretch and ended up inching around the fallen tree trunks further down. A young tree protruded from the ground; its branches weak against the wind. To its bark was a stapled letter with a kitchen knife pierced roughly through the middle.

Blade ripped it off, throwing the knife to the floor, taking a quick glance at the parchment. She opened it up and scanned the writing. Upon hearing the low wind whistle and the narrowing hooves, she pocketed it, turning around to see Oliver approaching on his horse.

"Everything alright?" he asked, reaching for a bottle of water strapped to the horse. He took a swig, offering it to Blade.

"I'm okay." Her head turned towards the castle in the distance. "I think whoever killed Aylie came from the castle," she muttered to distract Oliver.

She tugged her elbows together, feeling the parchment fold quietly against her ribcage. With it, a heavy weight settled on her chest and her mind wandered to the words she had read. It explained everything she needed to know.

"This whole trip was for nothing," snapped Blade.

"At least we know that now," Oliver replied in a calm and reassuring voice. "Don't worry about it. We have bigger things to take care of. I'm going to head over to the Crossroads, check on a few people. Coming with me?"

"No, there's one more thing I need to do tonight."

"I'll be at home if you need me. I'll head back north tomorrow."

"I'll see you there." Blade gave him a small smile that didn't meet her eyes.

As Oliver made his way south to the Crossroads, he couldn't shake the feeling that Blade's demeanour changed. He saw a fickle of regret or disappointment, but no anger. From kicking the frame of the cottage to suddenly relaxing her shoulders and tipping her head down, he couldn't understand what had changed between the moment she galloped over the prints to stopping in the outstretch of land leading up to the castle.

He didn't want to question her. She always seemed to know what she was doing, whatever it was, and Oliver trusted her judgement. If she had wanted to tell him something, she would have.

After leaving the horse by the side of his house, he picked up his bag and walked by the small flower field. The neighbouring people hated when Oliver sneaked over the fence to snatch their sweet geraniums and stuff as many as he could into his bag. Lucky for him, they were nowhere to be seen, so he slipped out unnoticed, whistling as he went.

"It's Oliver!" he heard an excited murmur before the door opened and a woman pulled him inside, squeezing him tightly into a hug. "Where have you been, boy? We have been waiting for you for so long! I had baked you an apple pie, but *someone*," she grunted, looking over at her husband, "finished the last crumb. I don't have anything to give you." The woman shuffled, opening all the drawers and storage boxes to find something to give to Oliver. "I think I have some cookies in a jar somewhere," she mumbled to herself.

Oliver moved inside, emptying the contents of his bag onto the table. "How is your ear?" he asked the husband, leaning forward to assess the mild infection causing the ear to redden and burn hot to the touch.

"Better than last time, but still prickling," the husband answered. "More geraniums? Are you going to get into trouble for this?"

"I'll be fine, sir. The leaves will help ease the discomfort and aid recovery. Besides, I'd rather get into trouble for helping than watch the world go by."

The overly sweet scent of the geraniums was nauseating so Oliver wrapped them up in paper, stashing them to the side of the table.

"Thank you," the wife said, lifting the metal jar open and pushing it into Oliver's hands. "I remember the time when more people were like you, Oliver."

"I can hardly remember those times, dear," her husband chuckled, resigning into a rocking chair, the panels beneath him creaking quietly.

"Valeis was once beautiful. And I mean, truly beautiful."

"She means from within," the husband added, nodding slowly in agreement.

"Of course, I mean from within, that's where real beauty lies." She continued, "Drishti lived amongst common folk like us as if they were our brothers and sisters. Even though the kingdom always had a Drishti ruler, to the day that I can remember, none of us were ever afraid. We lived in harmony."

The crumbs fell onto Oliver's lap when he took a bite of one of the homemade cookies, placing the lid back on top and putting the jar away.

"It's lucky we're old," the husband laughed. "At least the Queen won't want an old man like me amongst her guards."

"That's the only positive I can think of," the wife said, taking a seat on the arm of the rocking chair, kissing the side of her husband's temple. "I don't know what I'd do without you, love."

As a gentle smile graced her lips, Oliver couldn't stop thinking of how soothing the love they shared was, fresh like the morning dew sprucing up the grass each day. Witnessing their interaction evoked treasured memories he shared with Ezme. From the moment they first met to learning about how stubborn and impatient she could be, but also gentle and passionate and caring.

"I'll be going," he said, dusting the crumbs from his lap to the floor, gathering his bag. "Make sure you keep an eye on him," he addressed the wife, wagging a finger at her husband.

The husband fished out a pack of cards from his pocket, waving it in the air. "I thought we'd manage a round before you go."

"Well...I can't say no to that, can I?"

Oliver sat back down, taking the cards and shuffling them.

CHAPTER 24

Minutes stretched and the rain began to gently *tap, tap, tap* against the finished windows in the eerie church. Nathe could see the gnarled silhouettes of trees outside if he stretched his neck.

A thick glow from the scattered lanterns, encased in rectangular iron bars, illuminated the murals downstairs, exposing Ava's creative paintings. Trees spiralled into the stars on a midnight-coloured glass. Every other window was covered with abstract shades in different shapes splattered across with no purpose or direction – until the next picturesque story showed another landscape and another, until there was a painting of a kingdom. It stood out. It was unique. A beautiful yet dreary castle that invoked both grandeur and an underlying truth of oppression, lurking in sharper strokes of its towers and peaks. It told a story Nathe didn't care for.

Sitting on the top step, the bottle he held was warm from the touch of his lips. His eyes were bloodshot.

His mind traced back to the events of last night. The moment he woke up and she was already gone pained him, even though he should have grown used to her doing things her way. It was one of the things he loved about her initially, but he realised she lacked the ability to stay in one place for long. She was a free bird. If he was to trap her and keep her within a birdcage, she would lose her voice and her feathers would lose their shine.

When Nathe woke up, he noticed Oliver's boots were wet from the morning dew. He shook the droplets from his laces and his eyes followed Ezme rushing around the kitchen to prepare oatmeal. There was only one bowl everyone had to share so they passed it from one end of the line until it reached Victor, and he replenished his breakfast with two more heaps from the pan.

Nathe was tying his boots, folding away Blade's shawls and blankets and putting them neatly on the armrest of the sofa. He rolled down the sleeves of his shirt, throwing his coat over one of the forearms. Oliver stomped his boots on the mat and crossed the room, his gaze falling over Nathe. Nathe broke their eye contact, briefly taking in his surroundings, noticing that all the girls were watching him carefully.

"I better go," he said, making his way to the door.

"We can share some oatmeal with you if you'd like?" Ezme offered. Although trying to appear impassive, Nathe distinguished a velvet, warm-hearted worry filling out the spaces between her words.

"Thank you, but I better…" He pointed at the direction of the door with his thumb. He then swung his leg over the saddle without turning around, his boots fidgeting within the stirrup for comfort.

The door creaked open and closed again. It was Oliver who followed him outside. "Blade said," he broke the awkward silence, scratching the top of his head.

"What'd she say?"

"I'm sorry to be the bearer of bad news, but she wanted me to tell you she wanted you gone before she was back."

"I figured that much out," he smirked.

The silence between them stretched uncomfortably until Oliver said as a way of parting, "See you around?"

Nathe didn't answer, although he suspected what it meant. It was a form of encouragement for him not to let Blade dictate the terms. In a way, he knew he meant something to her and that was reason enough not to give up.

Now, he sat all alone in an empty church. Roof beams were a series of carefully carved arches, interconnecting in eccentric waves. Apart from the ever-burning lanterns downstairs, there was a lonely light hanging down from the middle of the high ceiling, seemingly losing its shine, flickering dimly as if taking its last breath. In the dim lighting, the small scratch on the side of his chiselled jaw was barely visible, covered by a stubble.

"You're drowning your sorrows?"

Like a shadow, she appeared out of nowhere, stepping into the dim light offered by the lanterns at the bottom of the marble staircase. He didn't hear when the heavy door broke open, despite rusty hinges he'd forgotten to oil.

He cleared his throat before answering, "Something like that."

He extended his hand to Blade. As she walked up, he noticed the lonely light began to swing back and forth from the moment she entered the church, wind seeping in. A seesaw of uncertainty; swinging back and forth, casting weak shadows. She grabbed the drink from him, taking a big swig.

"Ease up or there'll be nothing left," he quipped.

"I came prepared," she said, unfastening the buttons on her coat and taking out a full bottle of liquor, throwing it to Nathe, finishing the remnants of whatever disgusting thing he had offered her. "Mine's much better. Higher shelf."

"I would never doubt that," he laughed, dragging his sleeves up to his elbows; the way he always did.

"If I can, I treat myself to the greater things in life," she mused. Then quickly added, "You'll have creases on this shirt."

The corners of his mouth drew up into a sly smile and his thumb circled the surface of the bottle. There was a calming allure in the spark of Blade's eyes that told Nathe more than needed to be said.

Blade arched her left eyebrow, blurting a question before she could think about it carefully, "Your sister?"

"Ava...She..." He looked past Blade onto the mural paintings he'd seen Ava fussing around for so many days and nights. "She did a really good job in here," he marvelled at her talent, but knew this wasn't what Blade wanted to know.

Blade scowled, giving the murals a quick and scornful glance before returning her interest back to Nathe.

He continued, "She finished up when I got back and told me that she'd be travelling south in search of new jobs. A change of scenery, she said."

"And you?"

"Me? What do you want to know about me, Blade?"

"I—" she stammered, not knowing whether it was the drink on her tongue causing it. "I just wanted to know—"

"I'm not going anywhere." He shook his head, meeting her eyes. "At least not right now if that's what you're asking."

"It's not what I wanted to ask. I could not…" Again, the words wouldn't come to her, she suppressed them, biting her tongue.

"Care?" he finished her sentence, nodding knowingly and returning his stare to the bottle. He gulped down a few sips in succession before she snatched it away from him. "You're right," he admitted, caving, then wiping his mouth with the back of his hand. "Impeccable wine taste."

A midnight bell called out, echoing deeply through the hall and then, only the rain seemed to be interrupting the silence, pounding hard atop the roof.

"I like what you've done with the place," she admired his handiwork.

Before improvements, the church was a decaying shrine, rarely visited by the common folk, and often a shelter for the drunk. Although what they were doing tonight didn't stray much away. The leaves were taking over the floors until Nathe swept them out, uncovering the lost shine of the marbles beneath. The windows were tattered with crumbling bricks all around. Nathe uncovered the flaws and made them into a thing of beauty. The wooden panels all around were carved into shapes of flowers, running along the ledge.

"Forget-me-nots?" Blade asked to which he simply nodded. "My favourite…"

"I know that."

The growing sense of dampness and a thick layer of dust were gone, replaced by a light, pleasant hint of sawdust. The only untouched part of the church was where a family of birds nested, cooing quietly in the very corner of the ceiling.

The drink wandered from hand to hand a couple of times. For the first time in a long time, Blade listened to the whisper of her heart, scratching and clawing at her chest until she finally let it out. Her fingers lingered on Nathe's hand as she took the bottle again, but instead of drinking from it, she let it tumble down the stairs, crashing and spilling out.

Nathe's eyebrows dipped, wandering from the pool of lost wine to Blade's mud-stricken boots, thin waist, the strings of her necklace disappearing underneath her top to her unwavering, blue eyes. Unwavering and completely unreadable. Even for him. Her thick lashes blinked, and she let him reach for her elbow, bringing her closer. She held her breath.

"This is not my solid ground," she whispered as his eyes lingered on her wine-stained lips.

"I remember otherwise," he said, bringing her hand up to his mouth to leave a small, burning imprint. "Come back to me."

Her nose picked up his musky scent. They had shared so many moments and memories together. It was never going to be easy to forget Nathe, and deep down in her heart, she never truly did. Keeping him in a small chamber, tucked away for safekeeping. A flutter of promise always ready to extend its wings and fly right out, despite the cage being woven with heavy, seemingly unbreakable shackles. He was within her reach, but she was scared to extend her hand to him.

Words failed her, again, and she ebbed away from his touch, watching as his palm fell heavily atop his lap in quiet frustration.

He stuffed his hands into the pockets of his trousers, shrugging noncommittally. "I don't know what you want me to do."

Blade reached for her back pocket, fishing out a silver coin. "The head with a crown emblem or pointy tower peaks?"

"You mean heads or tails?"

"Isn't that what I just said?" she teased him, failing to make him smile.

He leaned against the balustrade with his back, extending his leg in front and bringing the other leg closer to his chest on the step below, resting his arm atop.

"Tails," he decided.

Fast, she spun the coin in her fingers, tossed it up with her thumb and it fell back into her palm. She covered it up with her other hand before revealing what it landed on.

"If it's heads, we kiss," she blurted as if deciding their fate was a burden of an inanimate silver coin.

"If I knew what was at stake, I would have considered my choices a lot more carefully," he joked although his eyes stayed pinpointed on her every move, the slightest rise of her chest with every breath she took, which seemed to become shallower with each passing moment.

"If it's tails," she urged, "what do you want?"

"Do you want me to tell the truth or something you'd want to hear?"

"Tell me something I'd want to hear."

"If it's tails, you take off your top."

She tried to withdraw her laughter, shaking her head at him. Nathe could have sworn the room lit up at the sound of her laugh, however cliché it sounded to him, he didn't mind thinking it and enjoying the sparse occurrence.

"Just tell me the truth."

"If it's tails, you have to come back to me."

She clasped her lips together into a thin line, considering his request. "I guess the coin will tell us."

"You have to lift your hand for that," he chided, trying to grab her wrist.

She stood up, driving her lower back into the balustrade on the other side. As she slid against it, the coat and the tunic underneath lifted slightly up and she felt the coolness of the handle against her bare skin, giving her goosebumps.

Nathe followed suit, standing right in front of her, his legs on either side of hers. He looked down, tilting his head. "Lift your hand up, Blade," he said.

Three pointy tower peaks.

"Tails," she whispered, looking up at him.

"I think fate wants us together," he said, a smirk appearing on his lips.

Blade slipped around Nathe, descending the stairs quickly. The coin fell from her hand and clinked against the marble. Sharp, metallic sounds.

Nathe picked it up, stashing it into his pocket. He said, following her, "Not again, Blade. I'm getting tired of you dodging me all the time."

"I have to go." She pushed the door open and this time it creaked, sending shivers across the hall. "It was a stupid game. We shouldn't have played it. It means nothing!"

He caught up with her outside, grabbing her elbow and pulling her close. The way he looked at her was urgent, almost hungry. It wasn't until now they realised the rain hadn't stopped. Blade's open coat hung very low, rain trickling down its end.

Nathe's hair clung to his forehead and Blade wiped it to the side with her hand, cupping his cheek. He pulled her closer, their wet bodies colliding.

His lips brushed the droplets from her lower lip, deepening the kiss the tighter he grabbed her waist. He broke away to say, "This doesn't mean nothing. It means something."

She pulled him back into a kiss by the collar of his shirt, her nails delicately scraping against the back of his neck until she heard a low growl in his throat. She didn't know when he picked her up and sat her down on a stack of crates outside the church, his hands wandering up her soaked tunic. Blade whispered his name in a quiet moan as he traced his lips down to her neck, to her collar bone, to her cleavage.

"Come...back...to...me..." he said every time he pulled away an inch to take a breath.

"I've always been yours," she said, "Just yours. Not anyone else's, but I must go, Nathe."

He returned to her lips, leaving tender kisses. He swooped her legs up to tangle around his hips as he pressed against her, the crates underneath her shuffled. "Don't go. Stay." The rain only intensified, tapping hard on every surface, breaking puddles in a frenzy to flow down the streets in small rivers.

"Let me come with you," he said, staring out into the night.

"You're not going anywhere. You're not a fighter."

"I can help in another way," he insisted.

"More people means higher chances of getting caught. I know that. You know that."

"I know," he muttered, tensing his shoulders.

"Besides, I don't want to give Hunter any more reason to come looking for you if any of this goes south. I need you to stay safe.

"Nathe," she whispered his name, pressing her wet lips to his cheek, "nothing ever happens to me."

He exhaled through his nose, putting his hand into the pocket of his trousers. The silver coin reflected in the moonlight as he twisted it around from heads to tails, tails to heads.

"I could have chosen differently," he mused. "But I chose tails."

The question hung heavy between them.

"You want it back?" He lifted the coin up to her, but she extended her flat palm out to him, refusing it.

"Keep it. I will be back in a few days."

He accepted it, pocketing the coin and turning to face her. She jumped down from the crates, holding his hands.

"I will be back," she repeated, meeting his stern gaze.

She tiptoed. And the kiss that followed was a hard promise. A much better promise than he could have asked for.

Nathe leaned his back against the crates, pressing his palms down on either side, watching as she walked away.

"Blade!" he shouted behind her. "Promise you'll take care of yourself!"

"I always do," she replied, not turning back, disappearing into the night.

The way she always did.

CHAPTER 25

Cassandra waited for Hunter to arrive at her chamber, but as the clock ticked into the evening hours, he still wasn't there. She sat in the armchair, tapping her fingers lightly on her knee.

The ticking of the clock drove her insane and she decided to sneak out. She failed to notice Hunter walking to her chamber from the other side of the corridor. Her hair flew loose behind her. He managed to see a flicker of the ends of her golden strands disappear from view. Intrigued, he followed. She looked back before she took another turn but didn't see Hunter lurking behind a huge vase the size of his body.

When she arrived in the hall, she left the door slightly ajar, trusting the marble flooring to make an echo if someone walked in. In the corner of the hall was a wooden piano. She sat down and lifted the fall board. Her fingertips froze in the air above the keys and she rolled her shoulders back, exhaling slowly. She hit one high key and then another.

Before the next notes filled every small hole in the hall in pleasant whispers, Hunter walked quietly towards her, admiring how her hands moved flawlessly over the keys. Sometimes she'd stumble upon the wrong note, only to quickly recover the balance. He approached closer and closer until he was right in front of her.

Cassandra's eyes were closed. Hunter found himself smiling at her, leaning against the body of the piano. He waited until she finished, leaving her hands suspended before she opened her eyes and jumped, scared at the sight of him. Her hand immediately cupped her chest in the spot where her heart was.

"What are you doing here?" she raised her voice. "I almost fell off the stool!"

"But you didn't," he smirked. He extended his hand to her, "Come with me."

"Where?"

"Trust me."

"It's hard to trust someone I know hardly anything about," she reasoned with him.

"Come with me," he repeated, rolling his eyes, his palm still outstretched.

She measured him before agreeing. Taking his hand, she stood up from the stool. "Where are we going?"

"Out through the main entrance."

"We can't do that." She stopped in the middle of the corridor just outside the hall, pulling her hand away from him.

"What your mother doesn't know won't hurt her."

"Well, that just about sorts everything out, doesn't it?" her tongue oozed sarcasm. "She always finds out and I'm not the one to contradict her."

"Stop living like a scared little mouse! Have some thoughts of your own."

"Aren't you just lovely," she snapped, crossing her arms. "Cass!"

Hunter grabbed her and pulled her behind the tapestry that hung from the ceiling all the way down to the floor, exposing nothing but their ankles. He held a hand over her mouth as she wiggled trying to shake him off. He moved further up to the wall, pressing a finger against his lips before he released his hand from her mouth.

"Be quiet," he mouthed, holding her hand in his.

Light steps travelled from one end until they quietened away from them. Hunter's hand felt cold against her own. She felt it drop from her grip as he peeked from the tapestry both ways of the hallway.

"I'm going," he said, turning back to her. "It's up to you whether you want to come with me or not."

"Lead the way," she muttered.

On their way, Hunter stopped by a broom closet, wedging the door open and reaching inside for a black cloak. "Put this on."

Cassandra's arms drowned in the sleeves as she buttoned it up all the way to her neck, making sure her legs were fully hidden too. While the castle gate was drawn shut with iron bars covering the entrance, one guard was on duty in front of it.

"As soon as the guard leaves the post, follow me out," said Hunter, leading Cassandra to hide within a shadow of an empty cart.

Hunter unlocked the small door on the side of the gate, pushing it open. The guard jerked, clacking his weapon on the brick wall.

"Just me," said Hunter. "Take a break, I'll take over for some time."

"Thanks, man," the guard replied, going back inside.

The evening was quiet. A few people with their heads down walked hurriedly across, a few stumbled on the path home from having a drink or two with their friends.

The hood on Cassandra's head covered her up and she held onto Hunter's hand as he weaved through passages in between houses until they found themselves in the lower part of the Blackwick town.

"I don't understand one thing," Cassandra pondered.

The roofs were slanted, some crumbling down, rain gutters stuck away from the grey weathered walls. The higher and lower part of the town were so different.

"What's that?" asked Hunter, pulling her further down.

Cassandra felt a chilling wind *swoosh* the hood off her head onto her shoulders. The houses were separated from each other, leaving an open valley running between them. Broken wooden fences trailed all around and most of the houses were pitch black, except for one that shone a feeble light in the distance. Cassandra squinted to see a shadow of movement inside.

"I was wondering, why don't you just leave? You have the key to almost everything. You're walking outside the castle gate right now with me. You could just walk away, and nobody would stand in your way. I certainly wouldn't."

Hunter chuckled, "You wouldn't? Why? Don't you want to keep me?"

"It's not up to what I want," she retorted. "Besides, is there a reason I should be wanting to keep you?"

"I could bribe you with a good breakfast. I'm not a half bad cook."

"I'm afraid, I do have a maid for that already," she scorned.

"And there I was thinking you'd grown fond of me." He gave her a smile, but not just any smile. There was a deeper meaning behind it, hidden beneath the boyish grin. "I wish I could leave, but I can't."

He stopped, letting go of her hand. Slowly, he pulled the hood back over her head, flicking a strand of her golden hair behind her ear. "Nobody can see you. Be careful, Cass," he said, his voice a deep rumble.

She wanted to ask him more questions, but before she managed, her hand was back in his. He led her to the side of a bigger cottage, the fence was cracked open for them to slide through and crouch beneath a window. Small slithers of light gave them a view inside from the drawn curtains.

"I want to show you something you don't see within your own four walls," he whispered. "When I was a kid, I remember how happy we were over a disgusting piece of cheese my parents managed to bring home once a year, if not less. I hated that cheese, but I learned to love what it represented."

Through the slither in the window, Cassandra saw a family gather around a burning fireplace, their hands extended towards the flames. Gentle smiles made their way between the father, the mother and their two children.

"They look happy," noticed Cassandra.

"They make the best out of their situation. Look around," said Hunter, "look closer."

The panels in the floors had holes and there were buckets spread across the room to catch rainwater from the weak roof. A table with a broken leg had just a single plate on top of it. A few crumbs left.

Judging from the woman's appearance, it was clear she gave her portion of food to her children. Her shoulders were bony, and her cheeks were hollow, skin an undertone of grey.

"Did my mother do this?" Cassandra asked, knowing the answer to her question, but hoping otherwise.

"Isla's reign is…" he paused, searching for the words. "Those people hardly eat and whatever they plough, if they have the luxury to be working the field, goes straight to the castle. I suppose a small crop slides into their pockets once or twice, but never enough times. The older son of this particular family is under Isla's compulsion and as long as there is hope, some families, if not most, will keep waiting.

"I hated that cheese," he added, both of his hands on the ledge of the window. "But there's a part of me that misses it." A slither of a ghostly smile appeared on his face and Cassandra understood what he meant. "People usually try to settle, despite the degree of how uncomfortable their situation is. They all hope for a better tomorrow, yet nobody does anything about it. They won't leave, won't search for better living conditions, because this is the best they think they can do."

"My mother…" Cassandra gulped. "She took you from your family," she uttered, placing her hand on his knee, making sure she was out of the way of the window for nobody to see her. Turning her shoulders squarely towards him, she asked, "What happened to your brother?"

"Initially, he hid in the attic," Hunter answered, shrugging his shoulders noncommittally. "He was lucky, or so I thought at the time."

She waited, but he didn't say anything else. "Hunter, what happened to your brother?"

Hunter stood up at once.

"Wait! Hold on," she said, standing up too. "Forget I asked. I don't have to know."

His arms tensed and his fists closed, shadows of veins on his arms barely visible in the night. It took a moment before she felt his calculated gaze settle a little. An hour later, Hunter was laying in bed, staring up at the white lace hangings surrounding the rectangular frame of the bed enclosure. Cassandra made her way over to her dresser, picking up a comb and brushing through her hair.

"How many times a day do you do that?" Hunter lifted himself up on his forearms.

"Twice a day. When I wake up and before I go to sleep," she answered, untangling a small knot near the ends.

"You pay too much attention to all of this."

She raised her eyebrow. "Weren't you the one that said a princess should be presentable?"

"I was joking." He rolled his eyes, taking a pillow from her side of the bed and stuffing it behind his back to rest. "You're beautiful no matter if your hair is a little out of place."

A laugh escaped her, shaking her head slightly. "You confuse me, Hunter. You say one thing and then another."

"Listen only when I speak the truth."

"Do you often lie, then?" she inquired.

"No," he said carefully, "I don't lie. I may twist the truth every now and then, but it's not a complete lie."

"Hmm," she murmured back.

"You're not so easy to read either," he admitted, watching how her nightgown folded over her curves in a whisper of silk. "Are you good or bad?"

She frowned, finding his gaze in the mirror. "What do you mean?"

"Are you a good person or a bad person?"

"You said I was just like my mother and even I wouldn't consider her good. In any sense of that word."

"Which one are you then?"

"People aren't good or bad. There's a missing 'and' in between. Nobody is truly either."

Hunter held her gaze in the reflection of the mirror until she lifted the comb up again and brushed through the second part of her hair. There was a blasting truth in what she said, and he had to consider her words carefully. It helped him make a decision.

"I *had* a brother," he began, his voice was steady, his composure stern.

A question of the past tense tugged at Cassandra's consciousness, yet she waited, swallowing an urge to speak. Her hand stopped halfway through a stroke. The comb made a soft *clink* against the dresser, then she twisted on the chair to look at Hunter. There was hatred painted on his face, in hard, rough strokes, seeping onto his tongue from every inch of his body.

"Your mother...She killed him because I didn't do what was asked of me. I was already a captor when he showed up at the gate looking for me. Foolish move," Hunter huffed, pausing to gather his thoughts. "He was Drishti and he showed up at the gates. I, of course, lied. Said he was a commoner. Isla was there and I prayed so hard for my brother to walk away, to leave me be, but he didn't. He wouldn't leave and when Isla approached...

"Well, she knew it right there and then – no matter what I would have said or done, it wouldn't have changed what she did next. She commanded the guards to grab him, take him to the dungeons and," he released a breath, "kill him."

Hunter dug his fingers into a pillow, almost tearing the thin fabric with his sharp nails.

"I'm so sorry," Cassandra uttered.

"He was supposed to survive. He was supposed to have a better life than I did. I have nowhere to run, Cass. I have no family left. There's no reason for me to try and run away if there's nothing I want."

His hardened expression weakened with Cassandra's touch on his shoulder as she sat next to him, leaning in. She pulled him forward and he succumbed to the warmth of her embrace, resting his chin on her shoulder.

"I don't want to be like her," she whispered against the nape of his neck.

"I won't let you, Cass."

CHAPTER 26

Ezme paced up and down the path leading to Oliver's house. They had to focus on protecting the children and everyone else, but the thought of their kiss lingered at the back of her mind and the conversation she had with Blade pushed her feet forward, sloshing through the residue of the overnight rain.

She knocked on his door. The hollowness of the sound held her breath. Different scenarios ran through her mind when she heard his steps getting closer. He opened the door. Khaki coloured trousers hung loosely from his hips and he wasn't wearing a top.

Taking him by surprise, as he staggered against the frame, she grabbed his face into both of her hands and kissed him. Before she managed to tangle her fingers in his hair, he pushed her away at arms' length. He searched her eyes and the muscles on his torso tensed up as he met her lips again, once, twice, for the briefest of moments, then slowly peeled away.

"Ezme…" he breathed against her lips, noticing how her small frame relaxed with his touch.

She held her finger up to rest on his lips. "No, don't say anything. I'm sorry, I pushed you away. I shouldn't have run away from you like I did. That's not me. I panicked with everything that had been going on. You, me, and then what happened with my father. My mind was muddled. I did what I shouldn't have done."

"Is that Ezme?" Blade's yawn reached them from behind the door.

Ezme's knees faltered, weakening beneath her and her arms fell heavy to the sides. "Blade?" she gulped. Her throat closed up, the air clutching at straws.

"She knocked on my door last night. I let her stay the night," Oliver said matter-of-factly. When he realised Ezme's expression changed and the corners of her mouth crumpled down, he added, shaking his head, "Oh, no. No, Ez. It's not—"

"No," she whispered, a slight frown appearing on her brows, "you don't need to explain."

She turned to leave, but he grabbed her, turning her around to face him. He was almost laughing.

"Oliver," she shook her head, "I should leave. I can't be—"

The door was pulled open wider and Blade leaned against it. "I told you she would come in the end," she addressed Oliver, a smile playing on her lips. "Thanks for the change of clothes," she said, tucking his oversized shirt into the front of her pale trousers, then pulled at the strings to keep them from sliding down her hips.

"Listen," she continued, sneaking around them in the doorway, "I got a few things to take care of. We need a carriage since we left everything up at my hut. I'll fetch it and I'll be back," she paused, quickly scanning Ezme's reddened lips, "either very, very late tonight or tomorrow morning. And I mean very, very late if you didn't hear that the first time."

She winked at Oliver, but before he took Ezme's hands and pulled her into his house, she quickly added, "Oliver, do what we talked about last night."

Ezme questioned, "What did she mean by that?"

"Did you really think that we—" he laughed. "Really?"

"Not every day I see you half dressed with someone else wearing your clothes."

A hot flush hovered up to Ezme's throat partly because of what she had just said to him and partly because he was still standing there without a top on. She went to sit on the bed.

"Ez," he said evenly, dragging a chair across to face her, its legs squeaking against the floor. "It was raining last night. All her clothes were soaked through. It's lucky she doesn't have a fever as it wasn't warm last night. She came straight from seeing that guy and needed a place to crash. Is there anything else?"

"No, no, you don't have to explain yourself. Even if you did, I had no right to question anything," she admitted, letting her chin fall down to her chest.

"I do have to explain myself to you because you do have a right. You have a right to my heart."

She laughed now, hitting him playfully on the shoulder. "Well, that was extremely cheesy! That's no way to get a girl."

"I made you laugh. That's at least a start."

"You always know what to say."

"I try," he said and grabbed Ezme's hands in his. "Blade wants you to practice. There isn't much time and we need to make sure you have a hold on your magic."

"Sure, the wolves are roaming around the edge of the woods at the moment."

"I don't mean the wolves. You need to practice on me."

"I can't do that. You know I only do it when it's the last thing available to get out of a sticky situation," she explained, backing her hands away from his grasp. "And you made me promise I'll never use it on you."

"If it's to help us, I change my mind. I want you to," he insisted.

"Right," she exhaled, pressing her hands on her thighs and raising her eyes to meet his.

"But before you do," he said, bringing the chair closer to her, her knees in between his, "there is one thing I really want to do before you get to see what's inside my head."

He slid his hand between her cheek and curls, pulling her closer. Her head twisted to the sound of wind chimes outside the window, swaying in the air. Oliver wanted to wrap her in his arms and never let go when her eyes returned to his, giving him a small, shy smile. The anticipated warmth rushed through him and he slowly leaned forward to meet her lips. He could feel her smile extend and when he pulled back, he planted a peck on her cheek.

"I'm ready now," he said.

Ezme took a quick breath in and, with an exhale, her eyes flicked momentarily grey, connecting with him. An image flashed before her eyes, reminding her of the day she feared she almost lost him.

"I have a small surprise for you," Oliver said, keeping his arms behind his back.

"Show me!"

He grinned, showing his teeth. "There are some formalities we need to get over first."

She rolled her eyes, hiding her face between her palms. "Alright, alright!"

He stuck his chin out to the side. She planted a kiss on his cheek after which she snaked her arms around him and grabbed the small package he was hiding.

"Ez! That's not how you should receive birthday gifts!"

"It is now!" She stuck her tongue out playfully, turning away from him and ripping the brown paper into shreds. The pieces fell onto the snow. "I don't know anyone else as practical as you are," she laughed.

"Well, at least you know there's someone looking out for you." He took her bare hand in his, her thin fingers cold and blue from the frost. Taking the gloves from the remainder of the paper, he put them on her hands. "That was only part one," he said.

"Are there any more pieces of warm clothing awaiting? Do I get a map of where to collect them from? Uh, like a treasure hunt!"

"One year older, one year stupider!"

"I don't think that's a word," she pretended to frown, crossing her arms.

"Shut up and come with me."

"Again, I don't think that's how you should speak to a birthday girl."

"We have to drop by my house. I made you a rhubarb crumble and stuck some pretty looking candles in it."

"You just spoiled my part two surprise!"

"You weren't going to come with me unless I told you."

The thick, hard snow crunched under Oliver's boots as he made his way towards the Crossroads.

She followed behind, arguing, "Still, the part three surprise would have been the hassle of getting you to tell me. You know, the whole, 'I'm not telling', 'Yes, you are', 'No way will I spoil it for you', to finally giving up, annoyed, and telling me."

"I thought I'd skip to the end,"

"So very thoughtful," she snorted, a smirk playing on her lips.

The door to Oliver's house was half open. Before he entered, he furrowed his brow to look back at Ezme. Inside, his mother and father sat at a table next to each other. His mother was in tears, muttering an apology, while his father's expression was firm and unyielding. Behind them was a Valeis guard. Oliver quickly scanned the room, realising there was a wad of money on the table before them and his mother's eyes were blemished with patches of sore red veins.

Oliver spun on his hill, screaming, "Ezme!"

A hand was clamped over her mouth and she was being dragged against her will. Her boots digging a deep, blackened path in the snow. She managed to slide her gloves off, then her fingers dug into the flesh of the guard behind, a warm trail of blood trickled down her palm, while she clung onto Oliver's distressed eyes.

"Leave her alone!"

Her feet kicking in the air, he was about to sprint towards her when the guard from inside the house followed. A swish sounded from behind Oliver as the guard extracted his sword from his belt. Oliver immediately turned and brought a fist to the guard's face. The sword fell, clinking metres away. Fist after fist, Oliver was hitting and hitting, until someone pulled him back, screams echoing in his eardrums. Before a sudden gush of pain on his cheekbone, he saw Ezme out of the corner of his eye, her hands tied up behind her back around a tree.

Oliver's tongue was soaked with the metallic taste of blood. The guard hit him hard. Multiple times. Until Oliver faltered, falling onto the ground. The guard's hands closed over Oliver's throat, eyes bulging out. He wiggled under the heavy grasp, weakening. The fight in him extinguished like a bucket of water over a small fire. His hand twitched.

And then the guard released his grip, falling on the ground. Oliver pushed himself up, wheezing. His bloodshot eyes met Blade's hardened expression as she extracted the dagger from the guard's head. The other guard was still there, his face swollen, brow split, lips a nasty, dark shade of rotten purple.

"Don't kill them!" Ezme shouted. "It's not their fault! It's not their fault!"

Blade didn't listen. Whatever remorse was within Ezme's heart was long gone from Blade's when she slid the dagger across his throat, gurgling blood out of his mouth.

Oliver quickly ran towards Ezme, untying her hands. "Are you okay?"

"I am, but you…" Her hand flew to the most prominent bruise on his cheek, then traced the cut on his lips.

"That sword is bloody," Blade noticed, picking it up. The hilt shone in the moonlight revealing a thick smear.

Oliver snapped his head towards her, over the long sleek finish of the blade to the still open door of his house. Regaining his balance, he ran inside and saw…

Ezme broke the connection. Reliving the memory gave her cheeks faint pink brushes and a sweltering warmth boiling over the brim of her skin.

There was nothing Oliver could do, except to hold his mother's hand with her last breath. Ezme never had the chance to thank Blade, and a part of her knew Blade was only going to perceive it as a sign of weakness. Something to mock. Nevertheless, she deserved thanks.

"We have no choice," Ezme said with finality in her voice, her expression unruffled, "we have to stop Isla's reign. It's gone on for too long."

CHAPTER 27

The castle seemed still despite the buzz of the chatter within its walls. It was the biggest day in Cassandra's life; her coronation.

The maids' uniforms were freshly washed, smelling of lavender fields. The guards stood around the castle's perimeter and even the stables were freshly cleaned, disposed of manure and the stench it brought. It was different. There was a celebration coming yet Queen Isla's steps around the garden were calm and full of authority, her head held high and her shoulders rolled back.

"Mother, can I ask you something?" Cassandra asked, plucking a petal from a rose.

Isla hummed, strolling over to rest her elbows atop the ledge of an arbour with sharp plants climbing over its framework. Rose bush beds filled up the square beneath. The garden was always brighter than the rest of the castle, at least in Cassandra's eyes, bringing a bleak sense of happiness. The soil was freshly renewed by the careful and patient hands of a gardener. The patter of last night's rain weighed down on the petals, driving them low towards the ground and giving life to new plants peeking through dirt.

Cassandra swallowed down a knot of panic as the question flew brusquely from her lips, "After my coronation, will I gain control over—"

"I will not be transferring my guards to you right away," Isla interjected, her voice clipped and definite.

Cassandra tried to hide the frown, turning her face towards the feeble sunshine, exposing blemishes upon her nose. Her fingers clasped the crown of the rose, crushing it together into a pulp, fingers stained the brightest of red.

"Oh?" she managed, keeping her tone light and breezy.

"I will first see how you do with a couple of guards before giving you more people to manage."

"As you please, Mother."

Cassandra smiled when Isla turned to face her, but as soon as she picked the hem of her skirt up to walk down the arbour's stairs, leaving her alone, the smile slid from her face and her expression hardened.

She returned to her bedchamber, taking the quickest path, trying to suppress her jitters by stomping her feet flat down on the new carpets she had received as a gift and pressing her hands on her knees to keep them in place. Everything seemed grander than any other day, however not in the usual sense of glamour and style, but in a heavy, thick, and suffocating overcoat resting on her shoulders.

She glanced out the window, through the rippled cracks in the glass formed by throwing her shoes at it with all her strength, onto important guests that walked past, dressed in perfect colours to celebrate.

She punched the window with the hilt of her palm, then pressed her hand against the cool of the glass, whispering softly, "If only any of you knew how hard this is."

"Losing your mind?"

She lowered her head and crunched her lips into a fake smile before turning to face him. "Good morning, Hunter."

His hand was hidden on his chest, in the folds of the cloak he was wearing over a patterned, elaborately woven shirt with dangling string below the nape of his neck.

"Talking to yourself is a sign of madness."

"Talking to yourself can ease your mind and help gather up your thoughts." She sauntered from the window towards him, taking the branch of small, white flowers he held out to her. "You should try it sometime."

"Cass…" The look in his eyes seemed to grow dim and dark. "You've been crying."

A lump curled tight in her throat and she blinked back the uneasy clamour wrenching inside.

"That's impossible," she laughed through heavy eyelashes. "Princesses don't cry."

Hunter gave her a long, hard look before wedging the door open and sticking his head through it. He made sure the guard that sat outside before he had walked in was gone. He then prodded the door shut with the tip of his shoe, looking down at her.

Her laugh ceased and she sat on the edge of the bed, nursing the branch in her hands. Accidentally breaking off smaller sticks and letting white cotton puffs fall to her bare feet.

"What's the matter?" he finally asked.

She shook her head. "Never mind, it's nothing."

"Well, it's something. You asked me to open up to you and I did. Now it's your turn."

"Hunter, I don't want—" she began, but stopped when she met his black eyes. "It's not how the tradition runs. I trusted her. I did whatever she told me to do, followed her blindly in all of her decisions, but she always brushed me off with the excuse that it will only make me stronger as the future Queen; that when the time came, she would be proud to give up her place for me. But she isn't going to."

Hunter listened, not saying a word.

"I've witnessed death as a common occurrence. I've led a life where I believed this was for the greater good. I've learned history from the mouth of a serpent telling me the land of Valeis is to be ruled by pure Drishti blood – our blood – and any other Drishti is an enemy to the crown. But they're not, they're not *my* enemies.

"I let it slide, many times over, biting my tongue when I should have spoken or done something – *anything* – but I didn't. You were right," she said, "despite not wanting to be like my mother, I did everything she wanted me to do. That doesn't make me any better than she is."

"You can still change that," Hunter said, walking slowly up to the window and running his fingertips over the cracks Cassandra had made. "You are going to be a great Queen."

"Without control I can't fix anything…"

"Leave that to me," he muttered.

She scrunched her eyebrows together. "What can you do?"

He shrugged. "I can think of a few things," he said. "But right now, we have your coronation and our wedding to worry about. I'll let you get ready and I shall see you shortly."

He walked up to her, to where she was sitting on the bed, and leaning forward he kissed her forehead. "Let's focus on one thing at a time, Cass. Everything is going to be okay. I promise you."

She stared at the closing door behind him.

CHAPTER 28

The air was still, peaceful. Blade slowed down, letting the reins and her hands rest on her lap as she inhaled the fresh notes of the woodland around her. Riding on a horse after a heavy downpour was one of her favourite things to do. She let herself watch nature bloom around her, from rosy leaves all the way to the mountains she knew were ahead of her.

A sliding droplet of overnight rain landed on the tip of her nose and her gaze snapped up to the overhanging branches with their thick, heavy leaves. Their barks were kissed with moss.

The hilt of her boots drove into the sides of the horse and it moved to a gallop beneath the canopy of trees until she reached an outstretch of land. Close to home. The peak of the crooked chimney was barely visible amongst the wafts of smoke warming the hut. The air immediately grew colder and as Blade breathed, curls of mist evaporated from her mouth with every exhale.

A rotting tree nearby was a feast for a woodpecker, full of insects to hunt, rocking back and forth with determination. Blade set her eyes upon the edge of the hill beneath which was her home, the same determination seeping under her own skin.

"Victor?" Blade called out from outside the hut.

The curtains on the carriage were soaked through as she ran her hand through them, checking on the two horses beneath a small shed. They were drawn close together with blankets over their backs, and heads sticking out over the fence, reaching for a stack of hay. She tied her horse next to them, securing the rope around the wooden pillar.

She pulled the curtains open and jumped onto the carriage, realising there was only one chained up barrel beneath a small hole for a window. She needed more than that. Crates and barrels, in their plural form. Something to hide within as not to stir any suspicion the moment they were to pass the castle gate. The space couldn't stay empty.

Blade heard the door swing open with approaching footsteps. Adie peeped, "He's out!"

She let her legs hang off the carriage, sitting on the edge. "When will he be back?"

"No idea. He went to collect more wood. It gets cold out here," Adie winced, screwing his face against the tiny amount of sunlight in between the hills. "Why do you live here?"

Blade smiled. "Offers solitude and stops pesky kids from asking so many questions."

"You like me," he said, crossing his arms.

"So sure about that, kid?"

"You took me hunting."

"And that constitutes us being friends now?" She raised her eyebrow, observing how his grey eyes extended over the horizon in contemplation. He bit the inside of his cheek.

"Yes," he answered, pushing his chin out.

She shrugged, jumping off the carriage. A huge frame of a man stepped into view in the distance. "Fine," she replied.

"Fine? It means we're friends?"

"Sure, kid," she laughed, walking past him and patting him on the shoulder.

Victor was carrying a huge piece of bark over his shoulder, dragging it through the hills towards the hut. Blade grabbed the back of the bark, picking it up and letting it rest against her own shoulder.

"Thanks," Victor huffed, his shirt drenched and sweat dripping off his nose.

"I'm taking the carriage," Blade said when she dropped the bark off, dusting the brown flecks off her shoulder.

Victor looked at her with a heavy sigh and gave her a nod. "When?"

"Tomorrow morning. Until then, I still have some things to take care of."

Adie climbed onto the carriage.

"Aren't you a curious little thing?" Blade appeared behind him and he jumped on the spot, scared.

"Why do you need a carriage?" he asked.

"To pack it up with goods to sell inside the castle," she answered half-truthfully. "Get down from there now."

She held out her hand to him and grabbing it, he jumped off, landing on the gravel beneath with a click to his ankle. He winced, bending down to massage his leg.

At the crack of dawn, Blade rode the carriage south to Oliver's house. "It's time!" she said, tapping on the window with her knuckles.

Blade, Oliver and Ezme made their way to the lower parts of Blackwick town. Blade knocked on the door until a man, not much older than her, opened it cautiously, peering around the frame.

"Is he here?"

"Who?"

"Nathe. Is he here?"

"I don't know who you're talking about," the man said, closing the door on her, but she pressed the side of her leg against it, fitting her boot into the open slither. She nudged the door wider.

"Get Nathe here, right now," she hissed. "I'm his friend."

Nathe stretched his arms above his head, stifling a yawn. "Morning, darkness," he greeted her. "It's alright," he said to the man who then scuttled back into the house.

Raising her brow, she asked, "Darkness?"

"You aren't exactly sunshine, are you?"

"That's actually flattering," she said, giving him a rare half-smile. "I need your help. I know you have connections when it comes to merchants and wares and we need barrels and crates and drapes and maybe rugs. We need to fill out a carriage."

"Anything else?"

"We need it fast."

CHAPTER 29

Hooves sounded on the cobblestones. Temptation to jump off the carriage washed over Blade and she tapped her fingers on her lap impatiently. A rug was covering her whole body and she was tucked in between two full barrels.

The only barred window in the carriage was small, dark and gaping, inviting to be looked through, but they knew they couldn't risk a peek outside. There were two watchers up on the towers on either side of the gate and a couple more guards by the gate, their eyes unblinking and expressions solemn.

"Don't," Blade snapped, snatching Ezme by her wrist when she extended it towards the window.

"I wasn't going to," she hissed back.

"We've been through this. If this is going to work, we need to stick to the plan."

The wheels rattled loudly on the cobblestones below and the carriage swayed, crates and barrels shifting from side to side.

"Quiet," Oliver whispered, interrupting their bickering.

The carriage stilled and they heard a soft pull of the drapes at the back.

"What's in this one?" someone called from the front of the carriage.

"It looks like…" the other replied, getting ready to step up, but he immediately wrinkled his nose when the stench hit him. "Or rather smells like…"

"Hunter! Check this out!"

Leaning against the gate with a bored expression on his face, Hunter picked his eyes up from the passing wheels and a hoard of people waiting in line to enter the castle. He had to vet anyone who was coming into the castle to make sure none of them were Drishti, while other guards made sure no weapons were carried inside. He had another hour to spare before he had to be by Cassandra's side, escorting her to the ceremony.

He cast a glance towards the rider, his eyes narrowing as he pushed himself away from the wall, approaching the guards. "What?"

"Something smells—"

"Fishy?" Hunter asked, distaste snarling his mouth.

The guards wallowed in laughter.

"I'll check it out."

The guards moved along the queue to the next people in line, laughter still on their faces.

Hunter's lips pressed into a line. He jumped onto the back of the carriage, immediately spotting a hilt of someone's boot. "You should teach your friends how to be less conspicuous next time," he muttered.

"Ezme?" Blade exhaled; irritation clear in her voice.

"At a guess, it's a woman's boot," he considered.

Blade uncovered herself from the rug thrown over her head. "The keys?"

"You only need this one," he replied, unhooking a key from a bunch tucked into his pocket. "I'll tell your pretty boy where to drop you off, but I thought I warned you about showing up with him. He shouldn't be here." Hunter shook his head disapprovingly.

"We're here for business. Put your job on hold and get over it. He's here as a rider. It shouldn't matter after we're done."

"Fair." Hunter saw a furry tail snake outside of the rugs. "In an hour, both Isla and Cassandra will be walking from the main entrance of the palace. You know, the place where you got caught last time," he sniggered. "All the way down through the square. I'll be there too. That's the best time to strike. Guard count should be low before then so station around. Don't hit a snag and keep your wolves at bay. We don't need any more casualties than necessary."

The curtains of the carriage swung shut and they heard Hunter's fading steps. He walked up to the rider, gravel shimmering under his boots.

"She saves your life and you decide to come down here yourself?" Hunter asked bemused. "I'd say that's a bold move, my friend."

"I'm in and out. Just delivering the goods," Nathe barked. "I don't know why she agreed to this in the first place…"

"There are things she would do for the right price and I managed to hit her weak spot," Hunter said through a grin. "You can leave the carriage over there," he informed Nathe, pointing a finger ahead. "Right outside the door so they can walk to the other side. In a couple of minutes, I want to see you leave through this gate."

Their eyes met. The veins on Nathe's arms pulsated. "It must really suck hating everyone, only 'cause you were the one to get caught."

Hunter grabbed the collar of Nathe's shirt, almost touching the tip of his head to his forehead, then with a deep exhale of frustration released him. Nathe smoothed out the crumpled shirt, taking the reins back into his hands. Hunter jumped off the carriage, watching as Nathe rode forward, stopping the carriage in front of the door, hiding it from the public's eye.

"You guys go ahead. Be careful and be quiet," Blade said, looking at Ezme. She wiggled the key in the door, opening it slowly. Before them, a narrow corridor led to another door by the end with weak sunlight shining through its bars. "Here's the key, I'm right behind you."

"Ashen," Ezme whispered, taking the key from Blade, and the wolf wiggled his way out from under the rug, sneaking through an empty corridor into the inner grounds of the castle with her. Oliver followed close by and so did five other wolves; one after the other.

Nathe made his way to the back of the carriage, walking up to Blade. She retracted her steps back to feel the wooden confinement of the carriage. He pressed his palms on either side behind her. Her lips parted to say something clever, but a sly grin replaced the need to say anything when he leaned forward.

The anticipation of the moment burst into pieces when their lips collided, when his hands found the small of her back bringing her closer to him, when he heaved her back against the brim of the carriage so far they felt it move beneath their feet.

He murmured, bringing his hand up to tuck her hair behind her ear, "You know where to find me."

She dropped her gaze to the floor, realising her clothes were starting to soak up the horrible smell. Nathe was already out of her sight, walking out of the castle. She made to jump off the carriage and follow behind Oliver and Ezme when a slight rattle from within a barrel made her head snap back to investigate. Blade lifted the lid carefully.

Nestled down was Adie. He stood up, stretching his small legs, his head popping out from the barrel, fingers curling around the brim.

"I wanted to help," he muttered, pulling his face into an innocent frown.

She gaped at him. Her cheeks turned pale as if someone had pinched blood from them. "You must be kidding me, kid," she gasped, drawing him up from the barrel. She walked up and down the carriage, then with one hand at her hip and the other cooling her forehead, she said, "I can't just leave you here alone. You're coming with me, but you have to do whatever I tell you. Do you understand me?"

He nodded, pulling down at the tunic underneath his coat. His hair was swayed upward in small, wayward curls.

Hunter told the truth, that's all that mattered to Blade to ease any worries she may have had. It wasn't a trap. As she looked around, there was nobody in the square and she assumed everyone was gathered on the opposite side of the castle where the coronation was to take place.

"He comes with me," Oliver decided, bringing Adie under his wing before Ezme had a chance to protest. "You can look after us with the wolves, but we'll stay out of harm's way. I'll take care of him."

"Fine," said Ezme, looking to Blade for further instructions.

"Take Ashen with you for protection, Oliver will take care of Adie, but be on the lookout to help them if they need it. Wolves are on standby. I'm going to scout the higher parts to find a good enough spot."

"What do we do?" Ezme asked.

"You stick to your quarters, making sure you have a clear view of me. I'll be the one to do it," she said, laying her hand on the dagger at her hips. "I need you to be on the lookout. If there is anything, and I mean *anything* at all, of danger before I can finish, we have the wolves to take care of it and your watchful eyes. Don't, under any circumstance, come down to the square when they walk through it. I want you to be invisible."

Oliver nodded, taking Adie and moving into the east wing of the elevated tower bridge. His and Ezme's eyes met briefly and she gave him a constrained smile, mouthing to him, "Be careful, Oli."

Ezme moved off to the west wing, stationing between two raised edges with Ashen, while the rest of the wolves stayed within the narrow corridor they had entered through. Blade grabbed the key to lock the door from the end where their carriage was left, leaving the other door unlocked for the wolves to be able to push through if they were needed.

Blade was to take the south wing, positioning herself in clear view of where the Queen and the Princess would enter from and walk south to cross beneath the arch.

They waited, time ticking and the sun brushing their faces with sweat. As the minutes stretched, Ashen walked along the ledge towards Adie. There was a door at the end of the tower path. Ezme was right next to it when it suddenly opened towards her, and two guards stepped in. In a moment of confusion, a guard pulled his sword out and thrusted it forward. Ezme managed to dodge it, her shirt slicing open inches below her ribcage.

"Ashen!" she screamed internally not to cause a disturbance, stumbling backward until she felt the coldness of the wall behind her and a nearing guard's eyes coming at her. "Ashen!"

Oliver's head snapped to her, as Ashen ran along the ledge from them towards Ezme. Ashen growled, throwing himself at the guard, but the guard managed to shake him off. The wolf's back paw was lifted in pain as he attacked again, getting a stronger grip on the guard's leg. The guard dropped his weapon and it clanked on the floor.

Oliver urged Adie to wait, pushing him within a small enough crack in the wall for Adie to almost fit in while he ran to help Ezme. He swung a clay vase over the top of the guard's head, causing him to fall down unconscious. Oliver dragged the man inside a crammed vantage point tower after tying up the bleeding guard, throwing him against the wall. Oliver ripped a piece of material, tying it around the guard's leg to stop the bleeding, then elevated his leg.

"You're going to be fine," Oliver said as the guard thrusted and twisted against the restraints, a muffled groan escaping from the gag.

Ezme kneeled beside Ashen. "Is he okay?"

"He'll be fine. It's just a broken paw. I can fix it later, but for now, tell him to stay here and not move. He'll only worsen it if he continues putting weight on it."

Ezme nodded, stroking Ashen's neck.

Their heads turned to where Blade was supposed to be. "Where is she?" Ezme asked.

The door to the palace swung open. Three guards stepped out lining up on the right side followed by three more guards on the left side. Queen Isla was the first to come outside in the procession. A few paces later, Princess Cassandra walked down the steps.

None of them saw Blade on top of the arch apart from Hunter. He had his hands in his pockets, walking slowly behind Cassandra, his eyes discreetly scanning the square. Minutes before they had walked out, Cassandra had turned to him, stuffing a single flower from the bouquet she was holding into the lapel of his waistcoat. "For good luck," she had said with a smile.

Blade lost sight of the Queen when her attention narrowed down on Ezme, her fingers winding around the hilt of her dagger. Her breathing eased when she saw Oliver running to help and her attention turned back to the procession, realising she had lost her opportunity as Isla had already passed underneath the arch. Cassandra was now beneath it.

Blade swiftly jumped down.

CHAPTER 30

Blade lifted the slick edge of her dagger to the hollow of Cassandra's pulsating throat. The slight rise of her brow and the intensity of her eyes dared everyone around to make a single movement. She felt Cassandra gasp and then hold her breath under Blade's slim fingers. It seemed like the whole world had slowed down and everyone was watching them. The guards around Cassandra half turned to the narrowing pack of wolves, their teeth threatening to kill.

"Now, now…" said Isla while flicking the guards away from her path towards Blade.

"Don't move!" Blade barked, raising her elbow higher. Cassandra arched her back and winced, her lips wobbling, fingers turning white from curling them hard into fists. With an angry spark in her eye, Blade continued after Isla clamped her mouth shut, awaiting, "Release the guards from your control and no one gets hurt."

Isla's mirthless laugh echoed in between the wolves' growls. "I really don't think you are going to do it," Isla responded.

For the steel to sink and draw blood it would have only taken a split second. Isla's gaze travelled to the far wall of the square and Blade's neck shifted slightly to follow it. She saw Adie but neither Ezme nor Oliver were with him. He was alone. One of the guards drew the boy up by the back of his shirt causing Blade to lose her focus, allowing herself to cast a longer glance in his direction, loosening the grip on the steel blade.

The world went silent as she felt a sharp pain pierce her shoulder. She staggered. Her fingers fought to circle the dagger harder. Another burst of pain shot through the side of her stomach and the steel fell from her grasp. Her knees gave way and she heard a familiar voice shouting, screaming, crying in loud bursts of panic break through the deafening silence.

Clanking noises filled her ears and her vision seemed to be curling black at the edges as she felt Ezme's warm fingers on her skin, delicately avoiding the arrows that had struck her, and helping her lie down on the cobblestones.

The air tasted warmer with notes of pine, reminding Blade of home, her true home where her heart was, and her cheeks grew pale, heat from them evaporating in curling mist ribbons, parting away.

An echo.

A simple echo split the cloud that seemed to have staggered her vision, blurring it.

It was his voice. She heard his voice, just calling her name. Faintly, but she knew it was him. She would recognise it anywhere.

It flashed before her eyes. Quick but real.

"You know what I like about you?" he asked her.

"No. Just tell me," she answered with a snap to her tone.

"Your sense of worth. You're not afraid of what anyone else thinks. You're your own person," he answered.

"Well, thank you, Nathe," she said, a smile escaping the confines of her armour.

"Do you know what I like about you?"

"Let me guess," he pondered, theatrically grabbing his chin in contemplation. "Is it my charming good looks?"

She shook her head.

He scowled, "Ow, thanks!"

"No, I don't mean..." she laughed, covering her mouth with the side of her hand.

"Don't cover up." He reached to pull her hand away from her face. "I quite like your smile too."

"Don't get used to it. It doesn't happen often."

"But always with me."

She turned, a smirk still playing on her lips.

"I like your voice," she admitted, but she could no longer hear it.

It was gone.

Just a feeble echo repeating in her mind.

I like your voice. I like your voice. I like...

And then she was back, seeing blood all over her hands. Panic and pain melded together in an agonizing dance. Her hazy gaze slipped, locking with Adie for a brief moment before it settled back to the person holding her. Ezme's face faded in as if through a waft of smoke, snapping into focus.

Blade tried to move, clenching her teeth together, but Ezme held her down.

A snarl painted on Isla's mouth. The wolves attacked on Ezme's command. The guards held up their swords to keep the wolves from jumping on them, narrowing closer together.

"Guards! Kill them!!" Isla screamed, then muttered under her nose, "An attack in my own house. How dare you!"

With Hunter's help, Cassandra scrambled to her feet, reaching up to her throat where she could still feel the coldness of the blade inches away from taking her life. "Mother! No!"

Her plea was ignored. Isla turned, furiously resigning towards the castle guarded in a circle. Adie was still suspended in the air, the shirt ripping on his neck, his legs flailing in amok. The guard holding him suddenly let go and the boy sprinted towards Blade, only to be stopped by Oliver's arms and dragged into his chest. Adie threw himself back and forth, trying to wriggle himself out of Oliver's firm embrace, but he only held him closer until he stopped fighting. Tears streamed down like a waterfall, clamping his eyelashes together.

Adie sniffled, finding it hard to take an even breath, his words muffled except for the prominent chant, "Let me go, let me…"

One of the other guards dropped their weapon. Cassandra's head snapped to him. She looked to Isla, then back to the guard, and then back to her mother again. Isla's knees faltered and she stopped, trying to support herself against the wall.

"Pick it up," she demanded, a feeble wheeze entering her lungs. She grunted, trying to clear her voice, but it didn't help. "Kill them."

Another guard dropped his weapon and soon all of them followed suit with the archers lowering their aim and laying down their arrows too.

"I demand that you…" Isla continued, her words dying on her lips.

On instinct, Cassandra ran up to her, fussing around, extending her arms to help, but all Isla did was slap her hands away. With worry turning into resignation on her face, Cassandra took a step back and then another until she felt Hunter tug at her elbow, pulling her towards him. He wrapped his arm around her waist, holding her.

Isla choked on a breath, gasping for air.

Her hand clutched her throat.

CHAPTER 31

Like an expelled breath, time had stopped and everything around quietened. Ezme held Blade in her arms, nursing her swiftly back and forth.

"Don't you dare do this to me, Blade!"

"You finally got your wish, haven't you?" Blade answered, wearing the barest hint of a smile, her voice weakening.

Ezme's memory flicked to their meeting in the barn, where she had said some horrible, hurtful things. "I didn't mean any of—"

"You did, sure you did. It's nothing new to me," she grunted, scrunching her eyes closed for a moment.

"Blade, I…" Ezme struggled for words, puffing her reddened cheeks.

"Listen," said Blade, "and listen to me closely." She moved her hand towards her chest causing a wave of crushing pain through her abdomen, trying not to look at where the arrows had pierced her skin. Feeling the arrows was one thing but seeing them would have made it too real so she kept her eyes buried into the disappearing snarl of Isla's features. She retracted her hand to a more comfortable position by her side. "Inside my chest pocket is a letter. Take it and read it. Everything is going to be okay now. We did it."

"What are you talking about?" Ezme asked, shaking her head, as she tried to ignore the strange emotions coming over her.

"Take the goddamn letter and my necklace! It's worthless now. It's done its duty." Blade coughed, a heavy, scratching cough.

A crumpled letter found its way into Ezme's hand and she looped her finger around the string of Blade's necklace, bringing it to the front of her blouse.

It was a rusty, half-broken key. She pulled at it, ripping it from her neck, then matched the missing piece to her own necklace her father had given her. It matched perfectly, falling into shape together. A puzzled expression sprung onto Ezme's features, furrowing her brows, her heart thumping wildly in her chest.

"Ez—" Blade continued, the last syllable of her name catching on another cough. She winced. "Tell Nathe...Tell Nathe I'm sorry..."

When all the weapons fell to the cobblestones, clunking heavily, Ashen trod slowly through the grounds, limping on his front paw, to lay beside Blade, covering her body with his fur. His wet nose poked her hand, shuffling his head underneath it. She stroked him. Ezme ordered all of the other wolves to join him, to keep Blade warm and comfortable.

Oliver let Adie loose and the boy took a shaky step forward, his face a mass of dried tears. He snatched Blade's dagger that had fallen from her hand, pocketing it. He kneeled next to Ezme, his wide eyes watching how Blade's motionless body lay on the cold ground. Ezme embraced him. The trembling of his small body was similar to her own, except for the terror in his misty eyes. The terror ceased from hers, not quite sure what she was feeling; fear, rage, angst, sadness…

Queen Isla dropped onto the floor not far from them. The guards succumbed beyond the arch, away from where the wolves gathered up. Some of them left the castle walls, taking their opportunity to finally be free, some of them stayed and watched. Nobody was kneeling beside Isla. She was quite alone. Cassandra pushed past Hunter's embrace, merely looming over her mother.

"She's dead," she muttered hysterically, "and it doesn't bother me…It doesn't bother me!"

"Cass," said Hunter, reaching out to her again.

"That poor girl," she said, turning to see auburn hair and blue eyes staring out into the sky. "Why do I feel more for her than for my own mother?" Cassandra's voice crumbled, her eyes searching Hunter's for answers, for comfort, for anything.

"All of this was for the greater good," Hunter said simply.

Cassandra's brow perked up in question. "What do you mean?"

"Blade was helping me."

Oliver and Ezme's attention turned to them while Ezme rested her head atop Adie's, soothing his sobs with a gentle caress of his hair.

"What did you say?" Ezme asked, recognising Hunter's face from the time they met at the castle gate.

Hunter acknowledged her, but his slim shoulders squared up on Cassandra. "Isla was going to die today. One way or another. Blade was a sacrifice."

Cassandra couldn't control what she did next. Her hand lifted and before she knew it, she slapped him. A sore, pulsating red patch welcomed his cheek and he kept his head slanted down to the side. He grabbed his chin with his hand and moved his jaw, turning back to face her.

"Blade knew what she was doing. She was either going to kill Isla or die trying, but her death would amount to this moment right now. A victory."

Ezme stood up, walking up to Hunter with hatred displayed clear in her eyes. If only looks could kill he would be dead. He held out both his hands to her, stopping her from advancing further.

He told her, "Read the letter."

With trembling hands, she pushed the letter against Oliver's chest. He took it from her, opening it. His gaze widened as he skimmed through the letter. With his other hand, he grabbed Ezme's, feeling how her fingers wound tighter.

"What? What does it say?" Cassandra asked, confusion and worry lacing her voice.

When Oliver didn't acknowledge her, she tried to step forward, but Hunter held her back. Ezme's gaze snagged and softened on Cassandra's face long enough for her to see understanding swirling within the depths of her eyes. Ezme then slid her gaze to lock with Oliver's before giving him a slight nod. With the first sentence, he pulled her towards him, and she rested her head on his chest, listening to his words.

Dear Akela,

I know you'll never forgive me for what I had done, but who knows what Isla would have done with your powers. I wasn't the one to risk it. She had done enough wrong in her life.

I had to do it; you must understand that. A father knows best, and you must trust in that as I trust what I had done was the best available option to keep you from harm's way and I consider it a success.

The night you were born, I took you. I stole you away, but could it really be stealing if you were mine? You were my daughter too. When Isla allowed me to hold you, she let her eyes rest for a moment too long and she fell asleep. Exhausted, right after giving birth to you. I merely saw this as an opportunity to run while you were in my arms. It was our only chance at keeping you safe. Of not turning you into a monster.

I found where Aylie lived. She was young and full of vibrant energy I somewhat lacked or suppressed deep within. I wasn't sure which one it was. I felt like I hadn't fully lived until meeting her. I came looking for a solution and she agreed to help. I could only imagine what she knew about dark ways of magic. I put your future into her hands.

"I need something she touched," Aylie requested, rushing around her cottage, picking ingredients from potted plants and dried leaves from rough wooden trays.

Within seconds the space filled out with floral smells, leaving a delicate taste on our tongues. I uncovered a necklace I wore, hidden underneath my dirty shirt. When I became a suitor, Isla handed me a key that opened all of the locked doors within the castle. She told me she wished for it to be a tradition; something to pass onto her future daughter.

I'd be a fool if I was to believe it to be a token of trust. When I touched it, accepted it, I could feel the magic in it. An underlying energy that gripped me.

"It takes an extraordinary amount of magic and an extraordinary man to be able to overcome the compulsion of the key," I heard Aylie tell me.

I listened intently to the explanations she had to offer while I rocked you back and forth on my lap with a hand placed over your stomach for support.

"The way my sister executed the spell allowed for a loophole. A suitor could not simply leave or run away, he had to stay, unless..."

She snatched the necklace from my hand, running her fingers around it. I could see an unearthed passion that took her gaze away, turning it into something I couldn't recognise.

"I need her blood."

Aylie pointed her finger towards you, without looking at you, and focused her eyes on the key as if looking for an invisible spell that cast it. I managed to look away when she drew blood from your thumb and all I saw were whirring drops, turning into all kinds of gory shapes in the cauldron. The floral allure seemed to wither.

As soon as you were in Aylie's grasp, you cried, twisting and pulling away as best as you could, but the moment you were back in my arms, you stilled and cooed against my chest.

"Unless what?" I asked, feeling how curiosity started to seep into my voice.

"Unless you had a reason beyond personal gain."

I thought about what Aylie said that evening. The reason I escaped was to protect you and to stop Isla from using your potential powers. I prayed, day and night, that your powers wouldn't extend beyond ordinary, if ordinary was a suitable word to describe any Drishti-born.

It wasn't until the discovery with the wolf that I needed to find Aylie and do whatever it took to protect you. She offered a way and I took it without a second thought. She unravelled the black string of my necklace and watched how suddenly the cottage became filled with smoke, huge darkening wafts escaping from the cauldron as she threw in the key that had made me stay all those years. The reason I could have never run away from Isla.

With what looked like a soup ladle, Aylie fished out the key and dried it with the bottom of her scrawny blouse, hurrying to kneel beside us. I wanted to reach out for the key, but Aylie swatted my hand away.

"You are not to touch this," she scowled at me. "The little one. Hold her palm out."

I tried my best to keep your fidgety fingers outstretched so Aylie could place the key into your palm. You immediately gripped it and when you released it, it tumbled to the floor in two pieces, cut right down the middle.

"It worked," Aylie sat back on her heels with a hand over her mouth. Our eyes met and I saw a glimmer of purity I hadn't seen in a while. "It worked," she repeated, not quite believing what she was seeing.

"I assume you've never done this before," I said, but as soon as I did, I chortled.

Of course, she hadn't. I watched her search and search within the many stained books on her shelves, some tucked away behind crates in stacks, a few recently used, sitting on the mantelpiece covered with just a tiny amount of dust.

I knew it came with a price to pay.

Nothing is ever free in this world. Magic or not.

Except…Except maybe one thing I could think of when my gaze locked with Aylie for a moment longer.

I picked up the two broken pieces and I could have sworn they still trembled in my hand, sending a weird sensation up my arm. I felt Aylie's hand encase my own.

"One of the pieces is enough to protect Akela."

"What about the other piece?" I asked, no longer feeling the sensation as something else took its place.

"It can be a keepsake if you want, but will have no magical value to you, I'm afraid. Only for her."

"What if someone takes it from her?"

"Trust me." Her hand left mine and the warmth quickly vanished. "The only way this key leaves her is if she gives it away willingly."

I thought long and hard about everything I had done and learned as I tucked you in for the night. With thoughts of giving you away circling my mind and not letting me close my eyes. With a bit of craftsmanship, I looped both of the half keys into a string necklace. One for me, one for you. In case you ever needed to find me, you would know.

With this sacrifice, I have given away your powers. You were no longer Drishti and just before you closed your eyes to sleep, I had seen them turn from grey to twinkling blue. Like the sky. No one would know you were once Drishti. You were safe.

But one thing that allowed me to go on was the knowledge that your mother could no longer hurt you without hurting herself. The moment she was to take your precious breath away, would be the moment hers would vanish too.

This was my protection to you.
Richard

Exclusive Character Art

Nathe and Blade

Oliver and Ezme

Hunter and Cassandra

ACKNOWLEDGEMENTS

I never would have thought I would get this far. If you're reading this it means I have pursued one of my dreams and this book is the evidence of: been there, done that!

There are so many people I would like to thank, but foremost, at the top of my list, is YOU! Yes, you! You who have bought my book, hopefully ended up enjoying it, have made my day as a result! PS. Tell all your friends!

To every reader, supporter, co-workers, friend and family member: without you no one would be reading this book, so that means you're very special to me and hold a place in my heart where I address all my heartfelt letters to.

To a bunch of wonderful people who had helped me with getting this book out to the best of their specialist abilities:
Three fantastic editors; Daisy Mumby, Kayla Grey and Morrighan Gregory, who have thoroughly read every word and when it was acceptable, gave me their thumbs up.
Ellie Lin who had created the most amazing sketches of my characters that I cannot stop staring at.
Autumn Krause who was there to keep me on track and never let me doubt myself even for a moment.
Paulina, Christina, Cass, Faro, Maha, Fede, Grant, Melis, Mert and so many more.

To ALL my bookish Instagram friends and followers who had been my greatest treasure and kept me going where the pages got tougher. Telling me they're waiting for it and that I had no other choice but to finish and give them what they wanted! The magic of positive peer pressure will never cease to amaze me.

Most importantly, to my grandad, Richard (guess where the inspiration for one of my characters came from? Hmm…), to my grandma, my mother and even my brother who I endlessly bicker with. But hey, brothers, eh? I'm also wondering, has anyone ever thanked their dog in acknowledgements for being there, under the table, scowling and scratching your leg to tell you they need attention as they're much more important than the book? Yes, that's Scruffy for you.

ABOUT THE AUTHOR

Ewelina Niecikowska was born on the very lucky 13th of December 1994 and raised in Poland.
She wrote ASHEN SHADOWS under the pen name of Ewe Linka. (Ewe is pronounced like 'eve' in seven)

At the age of thirteen, Ewe moved to England, then went on to graduate from City, University of London with a Law degree. Not quite the creative degree you may have been expecting, but she had always liked to dabble in many different things, such as her love for beach volleyball.

Her love for writing started off the moment she moved away from her home country where she would write long letters to her grandparents, telling them everything about her life and how she was getting on in the new environment. These letters then turned into something she would do every now and then to catch up in a written form on top of having phone calls with them.
Letters turned into writing short stories, short stories turned into writing elaborate grocery lists and, you've guessed it, elaborate grocery lists turned into writing this book.

She can be found online at www.ewelinka.net
Instagram: @iamewelinka

Don't forget to tag the author and add the hashtag:
#AshenShadows when posting on social media.